GW01418623

Welcome to Zimbabwe

By Arthur Gwagwa

©Arthur Gwagwa 2011

ISBN 978-1-908690-00-5

A Lion Press Ltd UK Publication

THE LION PRESS

Bromsgrove, United Kingdom
info@thelionpress.com
www.thelionpress.com

The right of Arthur Gwagwa to be identified as the author of this work has been asserted by him in accordance with Section 77 of the Copyright, Designs and Patents Act 1988. All rights reserved. No part of this publication may be reproduced, stored, or transmitted in any form, or by any means electronic, mechanical or photocopying, recording or otherwise, without the express written permission of the publisher.

A CIP record for this book is available from the British Library.

Acknowledgements and Dedication

I would like to thank Gloria Ndoro for using some of her quotes during our daily conversations and excerpts of her speech during the launch of Totem Shumba Estate in Harare. In addition I would like to thank her mother *Gogo* Ndoro, for basing the character '*Gogo* Ndoro' on her name. I would also like to thank my friend Dr Alex Magaisa for inspiring my usage of Zimbabwean English registers which helped me in providing a local flavour to some parts of this book. I also thank David Mungoshi for editing, Sarudzayi Chifamba for proof-reading, different Musicians whose songs I quoted and various unspecified sources that improved my knowledge of Zimbabwe. I dedicate this book to Zimbabwean children. I hope it will help them in being wise custodians of their cultural heritage and places of natural wonders.

About the book

Welcome to Zimbabwe is the story of a group of young people from around the globe who visit Zimbabwe on a cultural exchange programme that doubles up as a training experience designed to facilitate acquisition of life skills, cultural appreciation, mutual love and understanding. The 'Romantic Trio' from the United Kingdom enrols for the programme with a view to transcending their individual disabilities through cultural exposure and immersion in Zimbabwe. Through intense spiritual transportation Doug Cohen and Sarah Rhodes find meaning and identity while visiting Zimbabwe under the tutelage of two chiefs and an elderly lady called Gogo Ndoro. Initially, the group of visiting students is no more than a bunch of thrill-seeking young urbanites on a visit to darkest Africa, where they expect their worst fears and prejudices to be confirmed.

Chapter 1

Welcome to Zimbabwe

WHEN Doug, Laura and Kirsty arrived in Zimbabwe for their gap-year teen adventure, the warmth shown by the Zimbabweans they met at the Harare International Airport instantly mellowed their hearts. A throng eddied and sandwiched them in the airport concourse with their arms wide open in warm welcome. The local people extended their willing arms of generosity to help their guests at every turn, and yet they did not expect a reward in return. They had been born and raised up in a culture given to hospitality towards others. At the airport, Doug, Laura and Kirsty were joined by the rest of the students who had also travelled from different continents for this once-in-a-lifetime adventure. Since they were tired from the ten-hour flight, a Tenda Buses coach immediately whisked them all off to Zimbabwe's Eastern Highlands where the adventure began. As they went aboard the coach briskly with bubbling excitement, they could hear the driver's hushed voice announcing in a deep Eastern Zimbabwe Manyika accent, 'Welcome aboard this 2pm Tenda service to Chimanimani, calling at Marondera, Macheke, Headlands, Rusape, Mutare, and arriving at Chimanimani at exactly 6pm local time. Fresh snacks and cold drinks will be served on the way at the Halfway House.

1

We will also have a short stopover at the Christmas Pass for you to stretch your legs. Please respect Wasu, the bus conductor and trust me because we are the real deal *'Tisu anhu acho'*. After this announcement, the driver revved, stepped on the pedal and accelerated along the Mutare Road past the suburbs of Hillside, Rhodesville, Msasa and Ruwa. The soothing, mellifluous sounds of the Bundu Boys, Oliver Mtukudzi and Leonard Dembo wafted from small Samsung Speakers that were mounted on the roof just above their heads.

On arrival in the village, the Chimanimani Mountain stood there in all her majesty, as she had done since the beginning of time. As if in response to some mysterious pull, they all gazed at this big and imposing mountain. They tried in vain to imagine the memories it carried and what wealth it hid in its big, green belly. The mountain seemed to speak to their mellow hearts in a primeval language that made them feel they were back in the cradle of human kind where they belonged. They could never have been happier, or felt stronger and more assured than they felt on this day. In that moment of wonderment, the luminous summer sun smiled at them as it set cheerfully in this serene and sacred valley where the village nestled. In the sun's place, slowly elongating shadows formed and steadily encroached on the retiring village. The shadows of different longevity gradually merged to form a velvet blanket of darkness that covered the evergreen luscious valley. This process of nature continued in slow motion until the unsuspecting village was fully seduced into the valley's bosom.

For the villagers who had lived in this village all their lives, the sun's daily cycles and the shadows it created gave their lives some semblance of order. It demarcated their lives into days and nights. Its daily routines, behaviour and position in the sky were enough for them to tell what time of day it was, and what the weather had in store for them. If the sun hid behind dark clouds, they knew it would rain, but if it smiled in the blue skies, they knew they would have a fine day. To them, the conduct of the sun, the moon, the clouds and the stars played a very significant role in their way of life. The sun represented a divine manifestation of providence. As long as the sun rose and set, they knew that up above their heads there must be a God somewhere. Although they didn't see this God, their faith was very entrenched and so strong enough that they believed one day when they left their beautiful earthly inhabitation, they would go to that place where God was perched, way beyond the morning mist and stratus clouds decorating their skyline. On that day, they would cast off their worldly cares and burdens to be with their God. They believed that from behind the clouds, God relentlessly breathed the mist that engulfed the Eastern Highlands Mountains every morning and evening.

Their fortunes were closely tied to God who manifested himself in the elements and through the village prophets. For instance, whenever their wizened village head or chief gazed at the thin hungry crescent of the new moon, he could tell that the seasons conjured bad fortunes in the fields, while a full moon harbingered a good harvest. A cool breeze from Mozambique foretold a cold winter, but if it met a moist hot wind from the Hot Springs, they knew that a storm would brew. These people did not need a weather-reporter to forecast the weather for them because they had all the expertise among them.

The day the students arrived in the peaceful village of Chimanimani, villagers were seen darting up and down like deers, bringing their daily activities to an orderly conclusion. As the wheels of agriculture came to a graceful halt, they retreated into their enclaves for protection from the evil creatures and reptiles that lurked under the cover of darkness, ready to strike or cause misfortune. The village's clatter wore down and in its place came the hissing of night; reptiles, the humming of insects, croaking of frogs and chattering of small animals. The night owl perched exactly where the eagle had been perching during the day in preparation for its night vigil. In the pools, ponds, lagoons and water puddles, frogs jumped acrobatically into the dark and still waters as they hid under the lilies and turnips. The reptiles, squirrels and other mountain creatures left their enclaves and began prowling the fields, green meadow crofts in search of seeds, legumes and other edibles. The fireflies flew restlessly, providing points of light in the dark sky by supplementing the night stars; a few lamp posts in the village square, and sporadic flickering lights that came from the nearby housing estate.

The animal sounds created a harmonious night chamber orchestra of nature in the valley chamber. In the midst of this transition from day to night, some villagers could be heard

singing, 'Abide with me; fast falls the eventide; the darkness deepens; Lord with me abide. When other helpers fail and comforts flee, Help of the helpless, O abide with me'. After this, they would say a word of prayer before retiring to bed until the following day's third cockcrow.

The order and routine of this small village came to a sudden halt when the coach arrived carrying the excited students. The villagers who had not been told about this visit stood akimbo by the roadside watching the coach as it moved slowly before it stopped right in the centre of the village square. As the villagers stood there in amazement, Chief Nehoreka came out of his compound and issued a decree to his people that the visiting teenagers were his special guests, and urged his people to extend to them their hospitality. He signed a decree granting liberty of the village to the students. He could see that his people were becoming suspicious, because in previous years, scores of young European teen backpackers in gap years, had periodically 'raided' this village by imposing their cultures on unsuspecting villagers and sometimes posing as some sort of messiahs. Among the villagers on that day, standing akimbo, wearing a blue apron, was an old villager only known as *Gogo* Boriwondo, who began murmuring and complaining audibly as she said 'Hopefully these are not yet another bunch of white posh middle class sixth form kids who come to 'save' us without any preparation in political and social idiom, and who have not earned the right to 'educate' us'. However, her daughter, Amai Sekai assured her that if these youngsters were up to no good their

folly would soon be very clear like the autumn moon. She said, 'Ever since the beginning of this village, God has told us through the sacred mediums and prophets, of any bad things that would befall us. If these young people were messengers of the evil one, the prophets and the Chief would have found it out by now. Let's give them a chance.' Other villagers joined in the debate. Some of the villagers thought the students had come to explore diamond deposits in their backyard, in Marange, while others thought they had come to re-colonize Zimbabwe as one drunken man yelled, 'They are here for regime change. I heard their bus engine making a sound *regime, regime regime*, as the driver changed the gears.' He said this because the word 'regime' sounds onomatopoeic when associated with the sound of an engine. As the heated discussion continued, the Chief, who had disappeared into his house, came out dressed in full tweed and Wellington boots. In his right hand, he held a musical staff that resembled an orchestra conductor's baton.

'By virtue of authority vested in me as the Chief of this village, I invited these gap year students from all over the world for a month-long training camp in life skills and a series of musicals', the Chief told his villagers. 'Please relax and hold your peace', he added as he dispelled the suspicion in the villagers' minds that 'aliens' had invaded their quiet habitat. 'You will have a lot of fun with his young guests', the Chief spoke gently but with authority, and wit was written all over his wrinkled face. His charm and physical stature however defied all signs of

old age. He was as strong as an ox and as fit as a fiddle.

***

This training camp that was going to take place in the Chimanimani Village Mountains and other Zimbabwean areas of natural wonders was meant to equip the visiting students for life. There would be some spontaneous musical interludes and other forms of entertainment in the game parks and villages. At the same time, this was going to give the Zimbabwean communities an opportunity to showcase their greatness to the rest of the world. These students would go back to their respective countries with stories to tell about Zimbabwe's magnificent holiday resorts from the Chimanimani Mountains, the Vumba Mountains, the Victoria Falls, the Kariba dam as well as other places of great wonder and beauty. They would also be awash with stories of the ancient civilisation of Great Zimbabwe. It was the Chief's hope that this showcase would enable Zimbabwe to regain its reputation as a great country. He hoped that forgotten past glory would emerge once again and keep the world enthralled.

As soon as the Chief had made his announcement, his personally trained symphony orchestra strutted into the village square jubilantly. Local village cheerleaders, dressed up in Zimbabwean flag colours flanked the orchestra. They beat animal skin drums and gyrated to the sound. A curious throng of villagers stood watching and clapping their hands supportively. That day, the Chief's band

boasted of more soloists and an expanded choir. This band was called the Ngororombe and their music bore a similar name too. The Ngororombe had been played in this village from the 20th century, mainly by men using Shona traditional musical instruments which included the drum (ngoma), thumb piano (mbira), wooden xylophone (marimba), rattle (hosho), kudu horn (hwamanda), pan flute (ngororombe), mouthbow (chipendani) and voice (kuimba). The ngororombe was commonly played by a group of men standing in a circle and alternating ngororombe notes with lively chants and other rhythmic sounds. However, on this day, Chief Nehoreka improvised the music and expanded his symphony to include women. He rearranged the sitting and playing arrangements to ensure that the movements reflected the mood and tone that he wished to create during the period he was hosting his teen guests. His best soloist, Misha, rose up and began to sing sonorously a song based on Chris Tomlin's song 'Indescribable' in these words:

From the heights of the Zambezi to the depths of the Limpopo,
Creation's revealing Zimbabwe's majesty
from the caves of Chinhoyi to Victoria Falls
every creature unique in the song that it sings
all exclaiming Zimbabwe's indescribable and uncontainable beauty...

As the song went on and on, Misha was joined by the quartet of men and women. As this beautiful song came to a powerful conclusion, a

young man called Nakai began playing his *mbira* (a musical instrument consisting of metal keys which are staggered to a wooden board fitted into a resonator made from a wooden shell). He played it with ingenuity and in a way he had never done before.

In Eastern and Southern Africa there are many kinds of *mbira*, usually accompanied by the *hosho* (percussion). The *Mbira* is usually classified as part of the lamellaphone family. It is also part of the idiophone family of musical instruments. As Nakai played this instrument, he seamlessly carried on from where the choir had left as his trained hands relentlessly played the metal keys with an unmistakable stroke of a genius. The whole Ngororombe then joined in, building on the foundation that had been laid by Misha and Nakai, performing with high energy until they reached a triumphal conclusion. The opening mbira sound was arresting with its typical hammer blows. Chief Nehoreka had personally composed this musical piece after getting inspiration from a woodpecker one day, when he was searching for honey in the Mavhuradonha wilderness whilst away on holiday. He claimed that his God (*Musikavanhu)* had inspired him in composing this piece.

After the song, the combined African children choir rose up in unison and sang Henry Olonga's *Nyika yedu yeZimbabwe* (Zimbabwe our country). As they sang, several villagers were waving the Zimbabwean flag while young boys and girls danced acrobatically in a well-knit choreography in rhythm to the beat. In the

9

meantime, the visiting students had taken their seats on the terraces overlooking the square where the Ngororombe was performing. After the Ngororombe, Sekuru Gamanya performed a rendition of several songs by Sekuru Gowora and he did so with such a high level of authority and aura that senior citizens who were in attendance were inspired to join the fun. Some of them smiled exposing their purple gums while others defied old age with their unbelievably energetic dances. Several villagers and a few Zimbabwean white farmers who appreciated Zimbabwean traditional music joined them. Among them was Jim Latham, a well-known Zimbabwean cultural anthropologist who had carried out a detailed study of the African instruments and music, and made some comparisons of *Ngororombe* with Russian music. However a few villagers still thought that African instruments and music were associated with evil, and therefore they avoided attending similar events. From their view point, the belief that had partly been associated with their religious views would have been confirmed by the ceremony that day.

The visiting students were humbled and honoured by this resounding welcome. As they listened and watched, the emotional ones, especially the French, couldn't help but cry and let out hot tears of joy and gratitude. Although they were very far from home and even if their cultures were different, they discovered that there was more that united them to Chief Nehoreka's people than what divided them. Beyond their different skin colours and shades, they realised that they were all people who had emotions, passions and an appreciation for finer things in life. For Doug, who had a musical disposition, the opening and the conclusion of this village *ngororombe* reminded him of the symphony orchestra they had attended in London just before departure.

As Doug sat there, he was thinking, '*For the first time, I have realised that music has no colour and speaks only one language- the language of emotions, which has united us all here today even if I do not understand some of the lyrics. How about this debonair chief who is larger than life, where did he come from? Where did he learn all these skills that transcend cultures? Is he some sort of archetypal chief who embodies all that a proper chief ought to be? It appears this chief might have studied Beethoven's music or might also have gone through experiences similar to Beethoven's'.*

As he subsequently learnt, the Chief had gone through a deep communion with nature in the Mavhuradonha wilderness in the same way Beethoven was inspired by Vienna's natural environment. On this day, the Chief's demeanour struck a resemblance with the way other conductors in London conducted some of the most successful pieces but he retained his own cultural slant. Despite his advanced years, he led with so much energy like Dmitry Kitaenko.

After the performance, the Chief gave a passionate speech welcoming his young guests. 'I welcome you to the beautiful village of Chimanimani. Among us today, we have Doug, Kirsty and Laura who have come all the way from London. We have Sarah Rhodes from

11

Bishop Stortford in England. We have Troy, Paris and Demi who have come all the way from Hollywood. We also have Marco who has come from Spain. In addition, we have students from the Vienna Chamber Orchestra, Gemma from Stevenage, and Alicia from Hong Kong, just to name a few of our most valued guests who number about thirty, all in all. In a few minutes, we will be showing you your guest rooms, all the facilities and washrooms. If you prefer, you can go and sleep in the Chimanimani Caves under the watchful eyes of the guards who work in my courts. These caves are also very comfortable and this would give you a chance to have an interactive night with hyenas. You will not face the menace of the lions as they have gone to sleep by now. Those who work for me will take you through all the health and safety procedures just in case one or two naughty wild animals break into the camp, although this is not likely to happen. We have carried out a thorough risk assessment before your arrival.

'However, we will give you some whistles that you must blow if you cite a suspicious-looking animal trying to gain entry into the village square. I am sure one of my finely trained hunters who work in my Emergency Response Unit will always be on duty to restrain such trespassing animals. My men recently attended a refresher course on controlling and restraining wild animals in Guangzhou China; therefore they use the latest techniques that ensure public protection while ensuring that no harm is caused to the animal. I know that some of you have come from very far away lands, and some of you are on their gap year. Let me assure you that this, 'Training for Life' Camp is going to be a life-changing experience. My Council of elders who will be facilitating most of the training will take you through some exercises that will challenge your attitudes and values. Attitudes and values are like trees, they grow if properly nurtured, but can remain undeveloped if not. We will be focussing on this area through a series of challenging activities.

'We will stretch you like rubber bands. As you know, human beings are like rubber bands - *rhekeni* in my language - we are useless unless we are stretched. This is going to be your moment of personal growth. We will leave no stone unturned and will adopt a holistic and culturally competent approach in our training as we are aware that your respective needs may be diverse. For example, this is going to be your turning point in understanding the role of the arts and that of sound relationships in promoting mental health and well being as well as wholesome communities. Your experiences in this village and other places you will visit will not only be culturally enriching but will also equip you with life skills, which you will continue to use way after you have resolved some of the issues you might have had when you touched down on Zimbabwe's soil this evening.'

Chief Nehoreka continued, 'Before you go to sleep tonight let me tell you a little bit about this Chimanimani area from where your main training will be taking place. My co-trainers will tell you about other training camps around the country when you visit them during the course of this month that you are here. This village has existed ever since the beginning of our civilisation many centuries ago. However, in its contemporary state, a Scottish Traveller called Thomas Moodie in 1892 founded it. As you will subsequently learn, this village lies more than 200 miles east of Harare, which is the capital city of Zimbabwe, and we are in the foothills of the Chimanimani Mountains.

'From its inception and for more than a century our village has hosted various arts festivals featuring local traditional musicians. Early this year our art tradition has continued in earnest and we have attracted both local and international acts. We recently hosted Barcelona-based Spanish street performers Pa lo Q'Sea who use mythology, tradition, ritual elements and legends to realize a contemporary 'Fiesta' featuring recyclable large puppets, stilt-walkers, unicyclists, jugglers, drummers and acrobats.

'Thriving timber and tea plantations sustain our community and tourist industry that provides us with the much-needed foreign currency. I am very happy that your visit here will pump in the much-needed foreign currency into our local economy. Not many people in the village have nine to five jobs as you do in the Western countries and as is the case also in our cities. We rely on many streams of income that also include selling crotchets and other works of art to visiting tourists. We also do batter trading and set up money-saving cooperatives. We believe that this life style promotes good health. Our people are kept on their toes and are motivated by a mixture of activities that constantly keep them engaged.'

After Chief Nehoreka had finished giving his speech, his specially trained men and women led the guests to their rooms. There was a lot of excitement in the training camp as the guests mingled with the locals getting to know each other. Among the local children who were going to be part of the training camp were three teenagers called Misha, Nakai and Shona who had participated in the welcome musical and also Ndombo, Farai, Farisai and others.

***

At a time when the visiting students were busy preparing to come to Zimbabwe, the local children were equally busy preparing to meet them. Daily, they would gather after school to practice their *mbira, chipendani* and other instruments in the village arts centre. Nakai coordinated all the activities under the watchful eye of the Chief. Nakai's family was from the local Chimanimani area. Unfortunately he had been diagnosed with obsessive-compulsive disorder from a young age. Scientifically he was known to have a hoarding syndrome. This mainly led him to collect large amounts of fruits and twigs from the surrounding forests. When some local children saw him carrying twigs, they would tease him by singing the song *'Mwana wenyu kutakura tsotso sedhongi rakatakura uswa mhai'* meaning 'Your son carries twigs like a donkey carrying hay'. Having been born in this wilderness, on the wild edge where Zimbabwe meets Mozambique, it was not surprising; therefore, that he had developed a close relationship with nature and its healing powers.

15

It was reported that he was born right at the border of Zimbabwe and Mozambique and when the two countries found out about his musical talent they both claimed him to be theirs. When people asked him to give an opinion about his nationality, he always stated that whilst his heart remained in Zimbabwe, his eyes had a tendency of wandering into Mozambique.

From a young age, he also developed an interest in exploration and music. He sang and played his harp in a way that harmonised with sounds from the wilderness. His music was closely linked to his faith, a faith that ran relentlessly in his family. As he grew up, his talent also grew through relentless practice until he became a well-known genius of the *mbira*, harp, flute and drum. It was widely rumoured that one day when he was in the wilderness collecting fruits, he began to sing the song *'Sekuru ndipeiwo zano honai ndadzungaira'* meaning 'Granddad please give me some ideas, please look at my plight, I am struggling'. He appealed to his granddad because he had always seen him go into the forest to pray. Whatever his granddad did in the forests did not matter to Nakai. What he knew was that whenever his grand-dad prayed, God always provided for the family. This also prompted Nakai to follow in his footsteps. However, for Nakai, his granddad had also become some sort of god and ever since his death, Nakai's prayers were a bit confused; sometimes he prayed to God but sometimes he pleaded with his grand-dad in the same way he was doing that day. Besides, the traditional culture in his country had also taught him that he could reach out to

God by praying through a human medium. As Nakai sang, pleading for mercy for him to be healed and for his life to amount to something, he went into a trance and saw a prophet who just appeared from the Chimanimani morning mist. The prophet spoke to him, 'Please stretch your hand and open your palm'. Nakai obeyed and the prophet continued speaking to him as he deposited a shiny diamond into Nakai's palm and asked him to clasp it as he told him, 'Here is your talent and promise. You were born with a talent and a promise but it was stolen from you by others and through adversity. Hold on to it, from today people will not see your disability. Instead of hoarding fruits you will hoard people close to you because they will be following your talent'.

The prophet continued, 'Be a good custodian of your talent and use it wisely for the betterment of others. One day I will ask you to give an account of how you used your talent. Be a faithful and wise steward.' It is reported that from that day, Nakai became a musical genius and he began to command a huge following. His nightmare turned into a dream. The prophet was never seen again and his origins were not known, either in Zimbabwe or in Mozambique. He had no mother or father. He just disappeared into the mist in the wee hours of that morning. It was also speculated and even reported in the Chimanimani Chronicle that the day Nakai met this mysterious man was the day he regained mental soundness. The prophet had bestowed his blessing upon him and also healed him. When Nakai walked back home after the serendipitous encounter, he thought to himself,

'How many talented young people out there lost their talents through life's adversities? How many talented but disabled children are there out there whose disability has eclipsed their talent to the extent that they are referred to as so and so who is disabled? How many of them have lives that are defined by their wheel chair? What could be done to change that perception?' Nakai made a resolution to do his bit in changing this perception and he was going to play his part through his music.

Chapter 2: London

A WEEK before they went to Zimbabwe, what had begun as an ordinary evening out for Doug, Laura and Kirsty when they watched a play at the Barbican theatre would end up opening a tin of caged emotions that had been hidden in their conscience. Soon after the play, they all felt a ripple of raw emotions relentlessly welling from the bottom to the top of their hearts. 'We have to do something about this, We need to follow our lifetime ambitions to do something purposeful for the benefit of those beyond British borders', Doug suggested emphatically as Laura and Kirsty nodded sombrely.

When the play drew to a dramatic close and the theatre stage curtains slowly came down, the rest of the audience engaged in low-key conversations about their favourite bits in the play. At the same time, they were reaching out for their coats and scarves and fumbling for their purses and shoes under the dim-lit theatre seats. For some, it was just like any other ordinary day out. However, for Doug, Laura and Kirsty, the play's message on volunteering abroad had been forcefully driven home. Having been born and brought up as disabled children, their personal experiences had taught them how someone's life could be transformed through others' support. Ever since he was young, Doug had been diagnosed with obsessive-compulsive disorder; Laura had been diagnosed with a bi-polar condition and Kirsty had been diagnosed with acute clinical depression.

19

However, their lives were a living testimony that was timely and appropriate to those who needed it; in this instance other disabled children could help them to achieve their dreams. One day that recipient of help could grow up to be somebody and some day they could in turn help many others to also realise their life ambitions. The support that Doug, Laura and Kirsty had received from their immediate families, friends and school had lifted and set them on a pedestal of success. They were living their dreams despite their disability. Therefore, for them, helping the less- privileged was not a burdensome obligation or a charitable gesture but a calling, volition and a matter of social justice.   As they sat there, the play's epilogue began to sink and find a way from their head to their hearts. The main actor, Clare Finding, had closed the play with a passionate and motivational statement in which she said:

'At some point in our lives, we feel the urge to break out of our daily routines and explore the world beyond our comfortable confines. For some, this urge may lead to life changing experiences not only for them but for others too. We may find a sense of purpose and even inner healing when we leave our limiting confines. We can also make a huge difference to others in the process. I have read of people who ran gruelling marathons to raise money for cancer research, people who made life-threatening journeys to the North Pole to save the climate and even some who made journeys to the moon to advance the cause of science.

'I have also come across ordinary people who made sacrifices that might appear just as mundane, but that in turn made a huge difference to their children and communities. Some of the sacrificial acts, for example, involved parents moving neighbourhoods or countries to improve their children's life chances. No matter how big or small the sacrifices might appear to be, what unites, for example, an astronaut who goes to the moon on a discovery journey and an ordinary father who catches bus number 9 from Clapham Junction every morning going to work for his family is their willingness to make life-changing decisions. These decisions might be very unsettling but have long-term benefits. People who make these decisions defer immediate gratification for long-term benefits because they want to see future generations faring better than theirs. In the same way our generation sits on yesteryear's sacrifices, we also ought to sacrifice so that future generations have something to sit on.

'It is these sacrifices that help shape the world in which we live and that contribute to the perpetuation of human civilisation. Through sacrifices, these people inspire hope in hopeless situations and bring light which quenches a fear that could grip successive generations of people at home and in other nations. When we make sacrifices that inspire a sense of hope and raise the esteem of people who had resigned themselves to a life of misery, we empower such people to stand up and do something to change their life fortunes, courses and outcomes. In the process of helping others, and in our quest to change the world to be a better place for others, we often meet situations that challenge our own entrenched inner values and our embedded attitudes, which may in turn change us too in the process.

'However not many people will ever come to a point of realizing their aspirations of changing the world for the better. For many people, these ambitions will forever be unrealised aspirations. The ambitions might never find an opportunity for expression during the course of their existence. To you, I say please just go and do it today; there will never be a right time to do it than now. There will never be a time in life when we feel we have all the resources we need to help others because we don't give from the top of our pockets but from the bottom of our hearts. Thank you all'. A huge resounding applause followed Clare's speech as the lights came on.

During the following days, Doug, Kirsty and Laura always discussed Clare Finding's words. They had prompted something in them to awaken. Doug would end up being very obsessed about the issue, whilst Laura's natural kindness found an appropriate context to express itself. Although Kirsty was somehow sceptical about the issue during her moody times, she would display a burst of excitement whenever she was emotionally upbeat. In their daily journeys of coping with their conditions, they found something to relish. It gave them a sense of hope, meaning and a possibility to play a valued role in the world beyond their borders. During some of the following days, Doug would wake up during the middle of the night to express his ideas on a canvass using oil paints. He tried to capture the life behind Clare's words and the true sincere motives that accompanied them.

Although these teenagers had occasionally volunteered with V Inspired in Hackney and Lambeth, after the Barbican play they realised there was a great need for urgent help in other countries. They realised that love wouldn't be love unless they sent it on across the miles and the high seas. They had also been inspired by physically disabled children from war-torn countries living near-normal lives with a sense of hope even in the middle of trying circumstances, who were featured in the Barbican play. These children appeared to be blooming despite where and how life had planted them. They were like nice-scented resilient flowers in a field full of weeds. After watching these people's experiences, it became very clear to Doug, Laura and Kirsty that disability didn't necessarily mean inability. They also realised that there are many people with full eyesight but without a vision for their lives while there are physically blind people who have achieved a great deal in their personal lives and for their generation. For these people, disability was more a matter of one's attitude than their physical condition. The day one accepts and internalises society's label that 'once you are disabled, you are not able to carry out certain tasks', is the day that one indeed becomes unable.

* * *

For Doug, Laura and Kirsty, their opportunity to make a difference in the world beyond their borders and change their own lives couldn't have come at a better time than this although it eventually came in very unlikely circumstances. A few days after the Barbican show, they went through a World Travel Guide in alphabetical order until they came to the last page where there was information about a country called Zimbabwe. The Zimbabwean page contained a catalogue of interesting tourist destinations such as the Victoria Falls. They sought to obtain further information particularly to find out if there were exciting events towards Christmas. They quickly learnt of a place called Chimanimani located in Zimbabwe's Eastern Highlands. This place was well known for its mountains that were very ideal for climbing. In Chimanimani, there was a very wise African chief called Nehoreka who was excellent at empowering and equipping young people, especially in issues concerning attitude, thinking and behaviour. Coincidentally, he would be running a one-month camp full of fun, music and life-transforming training events during that same holiday. The event would also include an opportunity to live with ordinary Zimbabwean families in the countryside and at the same time volunteering for local village projects.

The three were very excited that their big idea of making a difference in the world beyond their borders was about to come to fruition. What they had not realised was the positive spark that would occur once their ideas met on a collision course with Chief Nehoreka's life experiences. Whereas they thought of changing the world in 'big strokes', Chief Nehoreka's life experiences would provide the fine details to their big plans. They didn't know that within their holiday package, something precious was hidden which neither money nor any riches would ever be able to purchase. It would be a holiday they would remember forever and an encounter with an African Chief they would eternally cherish. To them, the opportunity would only come once in their life. They cherished the idea of building bridges to link with less privileged children, exchange ideas on how to cope under difficult circumstances, and hopefully build life-long friendships based on mutual respect and interests.

What happened when these very kind and talented teenagers' life paths met that of the wise Chief who had a large heart and a vision for improving young people's life chances could only be described as a serendipitous collision course. When they were requested to give feedback on their respective and collective experiences in Zimbabwe, they were very overwhelmed with gratitude and couldn't find appropriate words to best describe the awesomeness of their one-month long experience under the Chief's tutelage. Being short of words, they simply gave terse statements about how they had been equipped for life and that they could best describe the whole tour as 'Training for Life'.

They had indeed discovered that way beyond its political turbulence; Zimbabwe had very active communities with very generous and sensitive ordinary people who demonstrated hospitality to their visitors at every turn. They would end up discovering another world of wonders, which had its own struggles, but was socially and culturally vibrant and so rich in many ways. There were many respectable and ordinary unsung heroes and heroines who loved their communities, and who were determined to bring up their children in culturally appropriate ways despite the economic and political difficulties. Although these people's names would never be written on marble or appear in halls of fame, they surely had a pride of place in the hearts of countless people whose lives they had touched. These people's small daily tasks and acts of resilience, hope, love and faith had strong parallels with Clare Finding's words at the closing of the play at the Barbican. They demonstrated that making a difference in our world is not only about carrying out valiant acts, but also resides in small acts of kindness to our neighbours and those who visit our countries. The people of Zimbabwe were not waiting for some grand utopian future. They saw their future as an infinite succession of presents; the presents which start by being seconds, then minutes, graduating into hours & then days. Therefore, they chose to live 'now' as they believe human beings should best live, in defiance of all that was bad around them. For them, this was itself an extraordinary and marvellous victory and act of heroism

***

When an opportunity to make a difference came, Laura, Doug and Kirsty were now seventeen years old although their compassionate vision for the world had begun early in primary school. People would subsequently come to wonder whether this trait was born out of nature or nurture. Laura, Doug and Kirsty had been born in Knightsbridge, Twickenham and Hampstead respectively, where they still lived with their families. From infant school, they had all excelled in different forms of performing arts. Their achievements, which were stunning, had far out-stripped that of their peers' and the expected targets in their key stages of development. During their formative school years, there was unconfirmed speculation that their ability to think creatively and experience a broad range of intense emotions in performing arts stemmed from their disability. It was suggested that their mood swings were a secret for their artistic successes. Consequently, they would end up having interviews with several British Psychiatrists who had hoped to discover new scientific truths from these teenagers' unique life experiences. However, their attempts to link mental illness and creativity had not yet been confirmed. Would their experiences in Zimbabwe confirm this?

Laura was a rising Ballerina and Choreographer. She was a very tall, slim and stunningly beautiful girl with green eyes and always carried a gaiety smile. Through her dance, she understood that dance could help her connect with her soul and force her to concentrate on the aspects of life that were greater than her immediate aesthetic world and brought her into contact with her God. This enabled her to change many things in her life. For example, when she danced, her soul and her brain were in harmony thereby changing her life and her reality.

Doug was an intense and romantic young man who had well chiselled features and a long nose bridge. He had an imposing figure, which was rather big for his age. He demonstrated a depth of feeling and imagination that gave the impression that he had been born to play the piano and to paint on canvass. He would always come up with some of the most imaginative paintings ever seen in London. He believed that both the brush and the canvas were simply instruments that had no consciousness. Together with the paint, they followed his desires and instincts. They conveyed his life onto the canvass and the contents of his soul. On the other hand, Kirsty, an intense and petite girl, was a great Soloist, Pianist and Violinist.

It was at Regency Park School of Arts and Music that these three had etched a reputation that earned them the name 'Romantic Trio'. They had acquired this name because their outlook of the world was revolutionary and their works of art was always different and carrying ideals of freedom and love. Their works depicted a world of conflict on the one hand, and of harmony on the other hand. Whilst they displayed pessimism in one breath, they also portrayed a world of hope in which all human beings would be equal and living in harmony as members of the universal human family. Although their works always led them on a warpath against some of their conservative middle class tutors who didn't believe in equality, they also began to gain prominence from liberal thinkers in the world of art who gathered at Hyde Park Corner and scouted all the London schools of music in search of rare talent. The liberal thinkers' philosophy was that,' stars are born, so let them shine, they may choose to shine alone or in galaxies, that doesn't matter provided they shine.'

It was not unusual that whenever Kirsty walked into an symphony orchestra hall and observed a nicely laid out perfect set of chamber instruments on the stage, she would muse to herself that, 'All of the world's nations are like members of a vast cosmic orchestra, in which each living instrument is essential to the complementary and harmonious playing of the whole'. In her mind, she saw some nations as violins, others as violas, some as cellos, others as piccolos, flutes, oboes, clarinets, bassoons, harps, horns, trumpets, percussions, trombones and tubas. She always imagined that if all people saw the world that way, there would be everlasting sweet harmony, with the creator being the conductor of this symphony. Those who tried to understand her thought pattern concluded that her Church of England values and her weekly mass at Westminster Cathedral shaped her altruistic views on the world. Ironically, Kirsty found refuge in composing music in her studio when her mood plummeted to low depths. In those times, she came up with ingenious musical pieces that she felt she could never have produced under normal circumstances. If she had been from a poor family, this would probably have been classified as irrational behaviour but because of the affirming environment she had grown up in, she always received affirmation from her parents for everything she did, something that consequently laid a sure foundation for a very successful

29

music career. For Kirsty, 'cattling' her strong and intense emotions into music was a coping skill which she found very effective in living with her disability. But would she find complete healing in Zimbabwe?

On the other hand, Doug, as a water and oil colour painter and aspiring architect, had a very ambitious view of the world. Art critics described some of his work as being wildly imaginative. He had a knack for portraying places he had never visited with exactness by relying on his imagination. When he read about Zimbabwe in a travel guide, he immediately started piecing all the information together until he came up with pictures that portrayed life as he thought it looked like there. He captured the valleys, hills, animals and birds as well as people going about their daily chores in the villages.

***

One day when Doug was standing on London Bridge, looking at the Shard, Heron Centre and other new buildings near the London Bridge, he conceived an idea of using art as an effective medium for bringing healing to the suffering nations at war or facing famine. As he imagined and carefully thought out this idea, standing pensively and gazing at the Thames waters, he imagined and marvelled as he thought that *Artists, like those scaffolds which are used in the construction of high rise buildings, should help in building a world which all nations can aspire for. Through our work, be it music, prose, poetry or paintings, we help others to progress and to achieve greater heights. We create objects of human aspiration because without artistic imagination, the wheels of civilisation would have come to a halt. I am saddened by the death of the 20th century romanticism that swept across Europe. Through it, the fabric of our society was changed for good; it prompted a cultural and political revolution. I believe that today's artists could also capture that spirit to fight human ills such as despotism, climate change, wars and famine.* He also imagined that *Although the human race has acquired a huge amount of expertise in building very complex structures, it still appeared to lack people who are able and willing to build up others through sound relationships that bring about positive change in the world.*

What made this Romantic Trio different and attractive to the London Liberal Artists and art critics was their ability to find inspiration from a wonderful multicultural and diverse world. They acknowledged that the world had become such an ugly place due to wars, deforestation and hunger, but they also envisioned a world full of promise and hope. However, as it subsequently turned out, their ideas, noble as they were, had not yet been subjected to a real life test. They would subsequently face the test during their visit to Zimbabwe. Their values would end up being challenged and their attitudes being subjected to rigorous multiple challenges. Furthermore, the wise Chief would end up giving them clarity on what the scientific community had been disagreeing on for years regarding their mental conditions.

***

31

On the eve of their tour, the Romantic Trio attended a philharmonic evening at the Royal St Albert's Hall together with their families. The event gave them a chance to say good-bye to their friends and to get inspiration and motivation for their world-changing adventure. As they walked into the well-lit hall, both Laura and Kirsty were elegantly dressed in short skirts and Doug was wearing a pair of lovely blue jeans that had traces of paint all over it. After being seated, the night began in earnest with uplifting pieces until it climaxed with Beethoven's Symphony no.5 in C minor, op.67. This renowned symphony was performed with high energy with its usual menacing opening and triumphal conclusion. The Romantic Trio listened, and sobbed with passion, emotion and sentiment because of their artistic, sanguine and emotional disposition. The opening bars were arresting as usual with their hammer blows. For Doug the opening and the conclusion of this symphony reminded him of a story he had read, that Beethoven's opening notes were inspired by a yellow-hammer's song which he heard in Pratepark, Vienna. The symphony's unremitting drive of the first movement depicted a dramatic conflict that only found resolution in the heroic finale.

That orchestral night helped the Romantic Trio to set the stage for their long-held great expectation to play a part in the building of a new world, a world in which conflict would give way to peace, in which strife would give way to wholeness, hunger would give way to food security, insecurity would give way to confidence. They were aware that this wasn't an easy task because there were many children and families out there in every nation that had something missing or broken and were seeking well-being. The Romantic Trio was prepared to do their best in building some bridges through relationships to help in building a world where human well-being didn't just remain an ideal and a wish, but became a reality in families, communities, societies and nations of the world. With the little ambition they had, and with hard work and determination, they knew that one day their artistic, idealistic and romantic vision of the world would come to pass. As they walked out of the hall, they were ready for their mission and they were confident that they would create ripples in the world. They were confident that through the power of artistic imagination, they could paint and sing into existence a world in which other children just like them would have a secure and confident future. Zimbabwe was just their starting point.

For the rest of that week the Romantic Trio spent most of their time attending medical appointments for immunisation, buying safari clothes suited to Zimbabwe's weather and terrain. They also spent time catching up with family and friends before they embarked on their epic journey. They weren't only excited about visiting Zimbabwe, but they were also thrilled about meeting other students from all over the world who were also attending the same event. All these were young people who had committed to lay a new and strong foundation in international relations. They had a non-judgmental attitude and didn't believe in the power of the barrel in resolving world conflicts.

They believed in the power of diplomacy and tolerance as the foundation in building a world that they would proudly call home. They were very glad that they could go and tap into the wisdom of Chief Nehoreka although they weren't quite sure how much this old African Chief knew about the world. On a very high note of hope and uncertainty, the Romantic Trio left England for Zimbabwe.

***

On the plane, the Trio sat next to a black Zimbabwean family. Most of the passengers were Zimbabwean families whose children had been born in the United Kingdom. There were also several former Zimbabwean white farmers who were returning home to try and get back on their farms after living in the UK for many years. The Trio had a map of Zimbabwe on their laps and were trying to figure out some of the places they were going to visit. However they were having problems trying to read or properly pronounce some of the names. 'Do you speak Zimbabwean, please?' Doug asked a boy who was sitting next to them. The boy just looked at them with a blank face until his mother intervened, 'He is my son. He is called Thomas Peters. He was born in England ten years ago. He speaks English and only understands very basic Shona, Zimbabwe's main language. By the way there isn't a language called Zimbabwean'. The Trio was even more surprised to find out that there was a Zimbabwean boy called Thomas, so Doug asked more questions, 'How come your son can't speak his own language?' The woman replied, 'It's a long story my son, we have been living in Brixton for ten years. I am sure you will get to know more about why so many Zimbabweans moved to England and why we have English names when you get to Zimbabwe.' A white Zimbabwean Safari owner who was sitting just behind them started to giggle and interjected, speaking in Shona, and offered to help. The Trio was even more amused that a man who looked like an English man could actually speak in Shona, whereas people who looked African could hardly speak their own language. The white man helped them by showing and giving them more information about Zimbabwe. 'This is the Chimanimani which used to be called Malsetter in Rhodesia, this is Kariba which is actually supposed to be Kariva, and this is the Vumba, a word that comes from *Mubvumbi,* or mist. This is Harare which means that people do not sleep there'. He went on and on, and his knowledge on Zimbabwe actually surprised some of the Zimbabwean black families sitting next to them, who hardly knew anything about their native country except their own village, or the high density suburb where they had grown up in, and the roads that connect the two. That was so much of the Zimbabwean paradox that the Trio could comprehend before they dozed off and only woke up when the aeroplane arrived at the Harare International airport.

Chapter 3: Chimanimani Mountains

DOUG suddenly woke up and began fumbling around thinking that he was in London. 'Where is everybody?' He wondered. He gradually realised that he had been dreaming and came back to his senses realising that he was in Zimbabwe. Although he suddenly missed home, his heart mellowed as he gazed at the warm sunrays of the morning that stubbornly found their way into his room through the slats in its thatched roof. He woke up and went outside where other students were already making noise, having lively conversations in the gazebo. They were waiting for the Chief to come and take them for the village orientation tour.

'What's happening here?' He asked as he joined the other students.

Nakai welcomed him and showed him how to play mbira. In no time at all, he was already striking some melodious chords.

'I am truly impressed by the weather. I bet in London it is very cold and depressing as we speak', Doug said.

'I cannot wait just to be out there and absorb all the sunshine,' Sarah added.

By the time they had woke up, *Rapoko* porridge was already steaming in big bowls neatly arranged on makeshift tables made out of reed. When they asked for some small side bowls, one of the cooks said, 'You will have to eat together from big bowls we have set in the middle of the tables. This is part of our *'ubuntu'* culture, which has run in our community for several generations.' After porridge, they had portions of organic wheat bread and frothy milk that had just been produced by the cows kept on the nearby farms.

As the students were still dragging their feet trying to deal with the jet lag, Chief Nehoreka was already jumping up and down, warming up for the mountain climb he was about to embark on together with the students. With him, he had hired his own fine men and women who would help him both with orienting the students and in carrying out the first training session. He also had a troop of dogs that accompanied him on some of these expeditions. He blew his whistle and beckoned the students to follow him uphill whilst a pack of his dogs and his co-trainers followed behind. In the light of the day, the students realised that they were on a mountainous area distinguishable by large, high peaks carved from a rifted quartzite block. Between the village of Chimanimani and the border, the ranges were more gentle and rounded. The national park was on the south of the mountain range and stretched towards the city of Mutare. Without doubt, Chimanimani had some of the finest mountain wilderness and also offered hiking opportunities. Close to the village they could see the scenic Bridal Veil Falls and a tropical rain forest, harbouring strelitzias, wild orchids, tree ferns, cycads and rare trees.

As the climb became steep, he encouraged the students to help each other along the way until they all reached one of the Chimanimani Mountain peaks where he sat on a flat granite rock, and spontaneously began to teach as if he was conducting a sermon on the mount.

'Hear me young people, I was once young like you but I am now old, and through diverse life experiences I have acquired wisdom'. He said so as he stroked his snow-white hair. 'One fundamental lesson I have learnt about life is that it is a journey that we should enjoy together with others. It is a climb like Miley Cyrus once sang. All of you are on your own journeys. You have taken this time-out during your gap-year to try and figure out which way your journeys would proceed from here. Please remember that although we all have different journeys, we still belong together as brothers and sisters in the universal human family. Do you remember how I encouraged you to help each other while we were climbing this mountain? In our life journeys, the relationships that we make along the way are far much more important than anything we could ever achieve. I am told that in the western world, relationships do not matter that much anymore. I am also told that you mainly relate through social networking sites. As you get older, you will realise that life is not a stroll in the park, but a tough journey, which is why I have chosen to begin by speaking to you about relationships today as part of your training. You will realise that you will need others both to achieve and enjoy all significant milestones in your life. Before you embark on any important endeavour in life, the question you need to ask yourself is, who is in my team? For example, your co-team may include your family members, a friend and your teacher. You know these people may never run away from you and will be there for you when you need them. However, you also need good relational skills to have other additional social networks of people to support you in other specific areas of your life. You could learn a lot on this from elephants. For example, in a recent study in Uda Walawe National Park, Sri Lanka, it was found that these mammals live in small social groups but they also maintain a larger, stable, social network. It was observed that some elephants were always seen in each other's company while others were 'social butterflies'. Only one in six of these elephants changed their 'top five' friends during the study. As you will realise later on in life, in college, your success may depend on what you know but after college, it will largely depend on who you know. My co-trainers will pick up on this topic again during the course of this camp because we all have to get it right the first time around, otherwise it would cost you opportunities to succeed'.

***

After the first session of the morning, Chief Nehoreka divided the students into small groups for discussion and group work. His co-trainers who included *Sekuru* Gora, *Sekuru* Gamanya and others were to help him facilitate the small groups. *Gogo* Boriwondo also came along to offer support and ensure that the sessions ran smoothly. She was now convinced that these students meant no harm to the village, but had clear intentions to have fun and learn about Zimbabwe. In one of the exercises the students were asked to imagine their lives as journeys and make drawings out of this, showing the beginning of the journey, major milestones, barriers along the route and the prospective destination. 'Imagine your life', the Chief emphasized. 'Reflect on the past and think of those times when you have been very happy and successful. Try to project that into your future. Think about where you have failed and draw lessons from those times. Imagine where you want to be five years from now, ten years or even twenty years hence. What epitaph would you want to see on your grave? Please write that epitaph now because it becomes your object of aspiration', the Chief added in a motivational tone.

Doug found himself in the same group with German and French students. The German Boys were also accomplished artists in their own right, having been educated at a Hamburg College of Arts whose foundations squarely rested on art, inspired by the haunting landscapes of Friedrich, the heroic panoramas of Koch, and the spiritual allegories of Runge. On the other hand, the French students also had wild ideas that had been heavily influenced by the ideals of freedom founded on the French Revolution.

What shall we draw guys?' One French student asked.

'Let us do a compound painting, some sort of portrait of a Great Zimbabwe', Doug suggested, using watercolours. His group agreed and the French boys were ready to unleash their wild artistry side like gazelles galloping on the Normandy valleys.

As they discussed the idea, a German student emphasised, 'As artists we have a moral duty to create a society people aspire to see. In doing this, we should demonstrate unbreakable courage following the tradition set by the German composer Beethoven, the writer Schiller, and painter Carstens who lived at a time when Germany was undergoing a political crisis'.

Doug added, 'Just like it was to Schiller, people could only achieve true and responsible political freedom when they had developed a sense of judgement that comes with an appreciation of beauty. It is our artistry duty to provide society with uplifting creations that would stimulate such awareness. I hope we could also do the same for Zimbabwe's beautiful people, some of whom have suffered unbearably'.

After conceiving that idea, they drew inspiration from Koch's famous 'Mountain view' painting as well as the lyrics from Chris Tomlin's and Henry Olonga's songs. They also got inspiration from the rising sun they had seen that morning, and other Chimanimani peaks that were within their gaze.

'We have to locate the source of light first', suggested one French student. In their picture, they portrayed Zimbabwe as a very huge park with a big mountain range that ran the perimeter of its borders. Within it, they drew rivers and creeks that criss-crossed ever-green luscious jungles. The rivers had huge deposits of alluvial diamonds and other minerals. On the eastern mountain range, there was a rising sun. In the centre of the country, they portrayed children and families playing together in harmony. They also portrayed waterfalls, a pride

41

of lions and other animals running amok in the green forests.

In the corner of the picture, right at the edge of the page, Doug drew three trees, one of which appeared to be bleeding, like an Indian Dragon's blood tree, the second one with shrunk canopy and the third one with small trees growing from its trunk. These were respectively known in vernacular as *mubvamaropa, tsikamutanda* and *gomarara*. He also drew a small mint tree and a dry fruitless tree.

When his group was requested by the other students to explain the meaning behind their picture, Doug explained, 'The Mountains represent a strong and protective leadership but also represent Zimbabwe's Eastern Highlands. The depiction of trees and animals in the picture represents a symphony of nature on the one hand, but also represents the ideals of harmony and tolerance that democratic countries cherish and enjoy. The wild waterfalls and storms represent times of civil unrest and political turbulence, but the fact that the waterfalls petered out into gentle streams signify the idea that storms and strife only last for a season, and that through compromise a country could live in peace and prosperity. This lays a foundation for building a just, safe and tolerant society'.

When the other students asked him to explain what the dragon blood and the other two trees represented, he explained. 'The first tree represents tears caused by suffering, the second one represents fear and the third one represents the burdens people carry when a country is not being properly led, for example, the burdens these people have to carry. However the mint tree represents the positive atmosphere that could be present if a nation is united through tolerance'. As it was, the other three trees in the grove were overpowering the mint tree.

'But you have forgotten to explain something. What does that dry fruitless tree signify please?' Misha asked. Doug continued to explain.

'In most cultures of the world a tree represents life. A tree is expected to grow, have green leaves, bloom, bear fruit and produce seed for the next generation. However when we eat all the fruits before they produce seed, it means the next generation might not have anything to eat or seed to put in the ground. In this picture I intended to portray the law of legacy here. In other words, I am encouraging the current generation in Zimbabwe to look after its wealth for future generations. For example, if you look at that tree, people who ate all its fruits were so greedy that they did not think about tomorrow. When they finished eating its fruits, they began eating its branches and when its branches were eaten, they began attacking its roots and that's what led this tree to be weary. It will never bear fruit again. I do not wish this for Zimbabwean children. Zimbabwean children are like oaks or the pine trees that you can see around here today. I would like to see all the children grow tall, straight and strong'.

The training facilitators were amazed that within such a short space of time, these children had produced such a wonderful piece of art that showed a variety of moods all bound together and kept in balance through artistic genius and sublime talent. The chief described it as a

43

painting with a deep moral purpose. He marked the words 'A Great Zimbabwe' on top, and took it to his house where he hung it on the wall.

Chapter 4: Mana Pools, Zambezi Valley

IT was a week since their arrival in Zimbabwe. They had already learnt a great deal from Chief Nehoreka's motivational Training for Life Camp. To reward their good progress on the course, the chief decided to charter a helicopter from one of the local white farmers to take them for two days to the Mana Pools Safari Park to watch game. The spectacular Mana Pools Safari is located in the lower Zambezi valley of Zimbabwe, very close to Zambia. The Mana Pools National Park is Zimbabwe's second World Heritage site. This area teems with wildlife especially during the months of June through to October. The park is popular for canoe trails as well as walking safaris, and is definitely not for the faint-hearted. Mana Pools is known for its abundance of enormous, beautiful trees that provide shade and make it ideal for walking in. The area is also known as one of the best places for walking safaris in southern Africa. The 'pools' which the park is famous for, provide permanent water all year round. This attracts an enormous number of wildlife. Close encounters with animals are quite common. The best way to explore this magnificent park is either on foot or by means of a canoe down the Zambezi River. The best time to visit the park is from May to October although temperatures can be fairly high towards the latter part of October.

Situated in the Mana Pools is the Chikwenya Camp which is rated very highly by many, and is regarded as one of their favourite camps in Africa. The students were going to be based there for two days. Chikwenya offers a unique location, incredible game viewing opportunities as well as expert guiding. The emphasis at Chikwenya is the serene Zambezi River, vast endless floodplains and the abundance of wildlife. The area offers magnificent photographic opportunities with tall acacia trees that dot the floodplains and the mountains of the Rift Valley visible in the distance. Chikwenya offers only nine tented rooms with en-suite facilities as well as an outdoor shower or bath 'under the stars'. Other facilities at the camp include a pub and lounge area under thatch. Meals are enjoyed outdoors underneath the trees or on the deck. The camp also has a swimming pool.

As the students' helicopter hovered above the Mana Pools Park, the young people could not hide their excitement. Through the windows, they could see the sparkling pool of water, a leafy jungle as well as various kinds of animals that dotted the jungles and the plains. 'OMG, we are going to have a good time here!' exclaimed Spencer, one of the students from New Jersey. One of the Zimbabwean students, Ndombo, from a local school in Chimanimani who had accompanied the guests responded, '*Ndakuudzai kuti muchanakidzwa* (I told you that you would have a good time'.

As the helicopter touched down on a cleared patch of forest, its turbines scattered foliage and blew up dust but this did not discourage the local children who were waiting to run to the exit of the helicopter to welcome their visitors. They

46

came from the local schools that had been jointly built by the government and a local Safari owner called Trevor.

These children then stood close to the exit and began to sing the songs *Nansi ingonyama bakithi Baba* [Here comes a lion, Father] and 'The Circle of life'. As they sang, the orange sun was just setting above the trees along the banks of the Zambezi River. The school prefects were in front to welcome the guests. Some local children were busy dancing, and Laura, Kirsty and a Canadian girl called Hannah joined these children and danced in sync with the local children's dances. There was so much multicultural harmony that it was incredible to think that these children were just meeting for the first time. As they were busy dancing, there was a stampede from a herd of antelopes, at very high speed. Just behind them, and within minutes, a pride of lions thundered past in hot pursuit. This frightened the young guests some of whom almost took cover back in the helicopter but Chief Nehoreka told them not to worry, as this was dinner time for the lions. As it turned out, sighting various animals either walking or running very close to where they were would end up being the order of that evening. As the girls and the boys were doing their choreography, a timid-looking buck stopped by and tiptoed as if it was imitating the dance. When the darkness began to intensify, there was less activity as most animals retreated to their hiding places. Rekai closed the session by playing his flute to the tune of the song, '*Mhondoro dzinonwa munaZambezi, Mhondoro dzinonwa munaSave*' meaning, 'The Lions drink water from the Zambezi and Save Rivers'. As he drew to the end of his song, Laura joined in with her violin.

In the jungle, the mighty jungle
The lion sleeps tonight
In the jungle, the mighty jungle

The popular tune brought the eventful evening to an end. The students were led to their lodges and tents for the night. Since they were properly guarded, some chose to sleep under the open skies watching the blue sky and the various stars that dotted the sky. Except for sounds from distant hyenas, owls and other night creatures, the night was peaceful and uneventful. Most young people were woken up next morning by the sounds of the birds and the warm sunlight that flooded into their chalets. They quickly took a shower and had breakfast in an open thatched lounge. The hearty breakfast comprised organic ostrich eggs, healthy goat milk, homemade corn-bread, and wild Rooibos tea. Fresh orange juice from the Mazowe Citrus plantation was also served.

After breakfast, Chief Nehoreka handed over the group to Trevor Davies to facilitate the training for that day.

'Good morning, I am Trevor. I am one of your hosts here, thank you for coming. I will tell you about my life as part of the training today, but could you please say out your name, where you come from, and state one thing you like and one thing you are good at'. As Trevor introduced himself, Doug had a feeling that he looked like the guy who spoke to them about Zimbabwe on the plane. As it turned out, Doug was right because Trevor had just returned from an overseas trip where he had travelled with a high-powered delegation led by the Minister for Tourism, on a mission to market Zimbabwean tourism to the British.

'I am Doug. I am from Richmond, a suburb in the South West of London. I am good at water painting, and I also like painting on canvass using oil paints too'.

Next in line was Marko.

'Hi, I am Marko. I am from Barcelona, Spain. I like playing football and that's what I am good at.'

Alicia Chan was next.

'Hi, my name is Alicia Chan. I am from Hong Kong. I like world languages, and I like writing short stories in Chinese and English'.

Then it was Ndombo's turn to say who she was.

'Hi I am Ndombo. I am from here, the Zambezi valley. I like playing my flute, but I am also a huge fan of gardening'.

They all introduced themselves. Trevor and his co-facilitators appeared eager to get to know each of the visiting students. One of the co-facilitators, a local Tonga tribesman, told them that he was good at hunting and his specialisation was chasing animals on foot until he caught them alive. When a gecko dashed by, very close to where they were sitting, the Tonga man went after it at full speed to demonstrate what exactly he meant. The students cheered him as he went after the gecko but he never returned to the camp. It was later reported that he had crossed into Zambia in pursuit of the gecko, which swum across the Zambezi. After the dust and excitement created by the Tonga tribesman had settled, Trevor resumed talking.

'Right, I notice there are students from every continent of the world. Right, eh, welcome to Zimbabwe. I am sure some of you had no clue where Zimbabwe was on the world map. This is it. I am glad you all came and I hope you have enjoyed your stay so far, and the training under the wise guidance of Chief Nehoreka. He is one of the wisest Chiefs we have in this part of the world. He is very tactful and has helped in resolving disputes between commercial farmers and villagers in the Chimanimani area of Zimbabwe. Okay, no politics here, we are here to equip you with the necessary attitudes, attributes and thinking skills that will empower you to choose your future career paths'.

'Sir where are you from? Are you Zimbabwean, too?' Kirsty interrupted politely.

Trevor answered. 'Yes, I am. I was born in Harare when it was still Salisbury. Harare is the capital city of Zimbabwe. I am sure you will have a chance to visit it as part of your immersion. I come from an influential family. In my teens, I played cricket for Zimbabwe and the Old Hararians, and helped my folks at the farm in Mazowe but decided to travel to see the world when I was eighteen just like most of you. I grew up with the likes of Duncan Fletcher and Byron Black. Andy and Grant Flower were my juniors in school. Kirsty Coventry and Charlene Whitstock are my nieces. Henry Olonga is a personal friend of mine.'

'Uhh, you are not serious, I know those people from TV. I thought they were English?' Kirsty said, suggestively.

'No, not exactly, that's what the media makes you believe. They were born and grew up here, but moved to England. I will not delve into their reasons for leaving since some of the reasons are political. The purpose of this camp isn't politics. You also know Chelsea Davy, Prince Harry's girl friend?

'Yes we do,' Kirsty, Doug, Laura and other English boys and girls shouted in unison.

'Her father owns a safari that isn't very far from this place, just down the river. *Uhh*', Trevor cleared his throat before he continued, 'Back to our main subject now. The purpose of today's session is to give you some tips on how to choose a career. I have been through it believe you me. I did my first degree in political sciences at the London School of Economics when my career as a cricketer was just about to peak. I then moved to Oxford and read Law. In the middle of my training contract to qualify as a solicitor, I changed heart and returned home to my ailing parents. I thought I would go back to London later but my heart fell in love with the animals and the soil. I have always been a son of the soil so to speak and very close to animals of the wild. I am told that my great ancestor was a hunter in Hampshire. It's not surprising that hunting blood runs in my entire family and through my veins. Although I undertook several other things when I was growing up, being close to the animals and tilling the land was so close to my heart that I had to come back to my roots and passion. I realised that my calling, life promise and talents were intractably linked to the soil, and to animals. I couldn't have fully realised my full potential unless I reclaimed my

51

God-given promise.' The students listened attentively as Trevor told them a bit about himself. They wanted to hear more.

'You see, everything we do in life has a reason and a purpose. There is no experience that we could ever consider valueless. All we do is part of our bigger and overall purpose, and contributes to who we become. You need to have the bigger picture in perspective whenever you find yourself doing small tedious tasks. However, having said that, it is also crucial to identify your main vocational route early in life because experts say it takes more than 10 000 hours of effort for one to become an expert in what they do. If you don't identify what you are good at early in life, it means that even though you might have bits and pieces of invaluable life experiences, you may never be an expert in any particular area. People are different I guess, some choose to be experts in one thing but others may choose the thrill of change. Am I suggesting that one should only do one thing? No, I am not saying that you should devote all your energy and time to one thing. Of course not! You can have other interests, for example, music and sport, but what I am saying is that in all those activities you may find it necessary to have your main career, which is in line with your most dominant thoughts, dreams, life themes, likes and strengths. This is what we are going to talk about.'

At this time, four boys from China, and a girl from New Zealand, began chatting in lowered voices, 'With all that experience he should definitely be able to help us. He should be able to tell us what we are good at.'

Trevor overheard the whispered conversation and responded.

'No! I won't tell you what you are good at and what you will eventually do with your life. That decision is entirely yours. My job today is simply to help you with some tools that will enable you to discover this on your own. A true mentor doesn't tell you what to do with your life, but through a combination of techniques, helps you to find the answers yourself. The answers are hidden right within you but require a bit of simple prompting.'

As soon as Trevor finished saying this, a woodpecker sat on a dry tree trunk close to where they were, and started pecking at the tree trunk and in no time at all; it had created a big hole.

'You see that woodpecker?' Remarked Trevor. 'It is good at chipping on wood and seems to enjoy the job and nobody ever commanded it to do what it does. If God can show a woodpecker what its occupation is, how much do you think he will show you his purpose for your life? I am going to put you into groups of two.. Together with your buddy, please, take a flip chart and pens. Divide the paper into four columns. In the first column put the heading, 'Childhood dreams' and in the second column, put the heading, 'My life's recurring themes.' And in the remaining three columns put the headings, 'likes, strengths and temperament, each in a separate column. Please work in pairs for this exercise, although I expect each one of you to have their own separate sheet.'

After that, Trevor asked the paired students to present their findings to the whole group and rounded off the session with a cautionary remark.

'Choosing the right career should primarily be determined by what you like doing, what you are good at, your personality and temperament. After this, one can, of course, take into account other secondary factors such as their previous life experiences, their original dreams and ambitions, parental influence, money and economic trends.'

Troy from the USA came up with an interesting presentation. He was good at following the latest movies and explaining them to his peers. He liked movies and he had a very imaginative personality. In addition, his father was a very influential figure in Hollywood. It wasn't difficult to predict that Troy would one day become a film producer.

After Troy's presentation, Trevor called for a two-hour break during which they drove around in an open jeep to watch animals. Trevor asked them to observe carefully how animals behaved as this would form the foundation for the late afternoon session on personality types. As the Tour Guides drove around, the students were filled with excitement. They had never been this close before to animals in the wild. Zoos came nowhere near this majesty.

A troop of monkeys threw some dry figs on them as they sat up on the tree. A male lion sitting on top of a big dry log and surveying the scene before it with an air of regency gave them a taste of wildest Africa. The herd of zebra and a few wildebeest managed to be relaxed and tense at the same time as they grazed and also kept a watchful eye on the king of beasts. Very close to the waterhole they saw a huge lone tortoise whose presence near the waterhole at the same time as less novel animals was conspicuous because it created an unusual coincidence. Some animals moved in pairs while others made their way to the waterhole in timid groups, always alert to the danger of predators that might be lurking in the undergrowth. It was fascinating to see how the different animals behaved, for example, how some animals chose to be gregarious in hunting for food and how others preferred to do it alone. The cheetahs hunted in groups whereas leopards did so alone.

When the jeep was at a close but safe distance from the waterhole, Trevor asked the students to disembark quietly. It was necessary to be as unobtrusive as possible in order not to disturb the animals. The day's session would end here.

Trevor resumed, 'As you might have all observed, different animals have different temperaments, habits and work styles as well as preferences. I will now try to give you an overview of how this relates to you and the issue of your career choice.

'One way of looking at this is to classify people as either extroverts or introverts. During our animal observation exercise you will have seen that the big tortoise was introverted in the sense that it was the only one of its kind present, and could not have had any interaction with species other than its own. The monkeys were clear extroverts, curious and playful. They chit-chatted a lot and appeared to want our attention. As you will also have noticed, the monkeys were in a compact and well-knit group.

By contrast, the tortoise was silent, practically immobile and appeared to be doing its own things. It was the slowest yet it lives the longest life. The question is, which of these two do you identify with? Would you consider yourself a tortoise or a monkey or are you in between? Please jot down your answers in the provided notebooks. Another way of looking at personality is in terms of thinking styles. As you might recall, we came across those flame lilies where the bees were collecting nectar for honey-making. The bees were very detailed in how they worked; they did everything perfectly and avoided making any mistakes. If those bees were people, I would call them 'detailed' thinkers. On the other hand, do you remember that leopard we came across? If you do I am sure you noticed that it surveyed the whole terrain, looked as if it was thinking of the future, and was always on the lookout for new stuff to do. In the local language they call this *'mutema rege wembada.'* That leopard looked like a 'big-picture' thinker to me. Do you consider yourself a leopard or a bee? Please jot down your answer in your books. We have other thinking patterns that we will not delve into because of the time. These include the 'logical' thinkers or 'follow- your-heart thinkers' as well as structured and free thinkers.

'In some cases you might have a combination of all these. For example, you might be an extrovert as well as a detailed and logical thinker or you might be an introvert as well as a big-picture and follow-your- heart thinker. These combinations can also lead to yet another classification of temperaments, one which sees people in terms of being idealists, theorists, and traditionalists, or live-for-the-moment personalities. Idealists often exhibit a combination of 'big- picture' and 'follow- your-heart attributes'. They are usually good at careers that involve dealing with people requiring a value-based approach. They can often be spiritual, emotional, people-persons and often lack practical skills. Theorists are usually a combination of 'big-picture' and 'logical thinkers', and love roles that involve planning and strategising. They are curious, visionary and competitive, and can have problems with authorities, especially if the figure of authority doesn't uphold standards that are as high as theirs. Finally we have traditionalist and 'live-for-the-moment' temperaments. Traditionalists love to belong to structured organisations. They respect rules and have a sense of duty to society. They can be inflexible and unimaginative at times. Traditionalists combine both detailed and structured thinking patterns. Live-for-the-moment people tend to be detailed and free. They enjoy each day as it comes. They are impulsive actors. They enjoy freedom and spontaneity. They are go-getters and can be practical. They don't want to follow rules but can be good in crises where they often offer practical solutions. They want to live life on the edge and easily get bored by slow and repetitive tasks.'

Troy, the American student, began to whisper animatedly, 'That must be my dad. He is both a pilot and an actor. He is a go-getter and lives for the moment.'

The session generated so much interest that the students began chatting about which type of thinker they thought they were, and what sort of career they thought would suit them.

'This certainly is training for life, Trevor. You have opened our eyes', Doug remarked with obvious appreciation. The other students agreed with Trevor. Trevor concluded the session by emphasizing the fact that what he had outlined were simply guidelines and recommended that those students who wanted to know more about this subject needed to have access to specific career guidance programmes and possibly do some psychometric tests in order to be fairly comfortable when deciding which career path to pursue.

He also emphasized other factors that one needs to take into account in career choice such as parental influence.

'Whilst it is not wise to sheepishly follow in your parents' footsteps, there are times when this can work well for you especially if your parents have expertise in what they do, and if you also have an interest in what they do. This can give you a head start in life.'

Trevor also emphasized that one person can go through multiple careers in life. 'For example, look at President Obama. He began as a Community Organiser, and then became a lawyer just before he entered politics. Who knows when he is done with politics, he might be like Jimmy Carter who volunteers with Habitat for Humanity? One's career doesn't end when they get old. You can begin to play other roles that help in making the world a better place. Career life is a cycle. You begin by learning, then go on to earn before you begin to return.

'If you feel that your nine to five jobs are not fully utilising your full potential, you can do other exciting activities after hours, for example, painting, pottery, fishing, the list goes on. The world is also changing and is increasingly demanding people who are multi-skilled and flexible. I am sure Chief Nehoreka told you that most of the people from his village don't work nine to five jobs. They have a fairly flexible and healthy life and work balance. That is why they are healthy. You also need to think in terms of being multi- skilled or even working globally.'

Trevor wrapped up the meeting amid a lot of excitement, and led the students back to the jeep before they retired for the night.

The following day Trevor took them for a day trip to the Kariba Dam, a hydroelectric dam in the Kariba Gorge of the Zambezi river basin between Zambia and Zimbabwe considered one of the largest dams in the world. The dam wall stands at 128 m (420 ft) tall and 579 m (1,900 ft) long. At Kariba dam, they enjoyed a cruise aboard a houseboat. When they disembarked the boat, they walked along a gangway that led them to the dam wall. Whilst walking on the dam wall, Trevor asked them to pay attention to the huge body of water that was held back by a huge dam wall.

'You notice how the sheet of water is held back or trapped?' Trevor asked them. The students acknowledged before Trevor proceeded, 'That's where the name 'Kariba' came from. It means 'trapped' because that wall is trapping a huge water body like a trap also known as

'Kariva' in Shona. However, you will notice that once this water is released under high pressure, it generates a high voltage of electricity.'

The students were fascinated but at the same time anxious about the point that Trevor wanted to make, because they wanted to go back for a cruise. Once they were back on the big boat, Trevor resumed drawing lessons from the way the Kariba dam generates electricity to illustrate the importance of recognizing one's potential, and how to release it towards worthy goals in life. 'Did you notice how the body of water only generated electricity once it was released through the dam wall? I would like you to draw lessons from this. I believe all of you have great talents and gifts but if you do not activate those gifts, then they will simply remain as unutilized potential. However, once you identify what you like, and are good at it and begin working on it, your potential will be released and this enables you to achieve your goals.'

'So is it like potential energy turning into kinetic energy?' Ndombo asked making reference to her physics lessons.

'Yes exactly,' Trevor answered. 'Just imagine how many people die with their potential? This might be due to lack of opportunities or even failure to take advantage of opportunities.' Nakai qualified this by telling the group how he was helping less-privileged young people in Chimanimani to realise their musical potential.

While most of the students were back on the boat, Troy and five others went on a guided tour in the Matusadona Game Reserve. This game reserve boasts a unique combination of pristine and rugged wilderness and the water frontage of Lake Kariba. It is one of the last remaining sanctuaries of the endangered Black Rhinoceros. It is commonly recognized as having the second largest concentration of wild lions in Africa after the Ngorongoro Crater in east Africa. Many of the animals rescued during Operation Noah when Lake Kariba was filling following the construction of Kariba Dam, were released into Matusadona, which now holds strong populations of most mammals occurring in the Zambezi Valley. Buffalo are especially prominent and herds of up to 1,000-strong, often congregate along the shoreline in the dry season. Troy and his team took very beautiful pictures using a very powerful camera, which they had carried with them. They subsequently posted these pictures on Facebook for their families back home to see the good time they were having. When Troy's mother saw the pictures on Facebook, she was frightened but Troy' father marvelled at his son's courage.

They spent the night in a yacht and proceeded to Victoria Falls the following morning.

Chapter 7: Victoria Falls

THERE is no better destination in Southern Africa, offering helicopter flights over the falls, elephant interactive safaris, game drives and night drives, walking with lions, river boarding, bungee jumping, canoeing, and of course the unrivalled white water rafting on the mighty Zambezi River, than the Victoria Falls. In addition, this place gives you the opportunity to interact with the locals, shop for souvenirs, and sip a 'Gin and Tonic' overlooking the magnificent waterholes where wildlife gathers to drink. You can also visit a local school, participate in a community project or eat local delicacies. The town has an abundance of food on offer: continental cuisine and local dishes that include dried kudu meat in peanut butter and cooked cornmeal (*sadza*).

Although Chief Nehoreka had explained how the Victoria Falls looked like to the students, they had not expected it to be this spectacular. As a tourism ambassador, the Chief had tried to explain using colourful words and expressions as he said, 'Whether you are looking for a five star restaurant or a café, Victoria Falls is the place to be. If you visit Victoria Falls you will meet warm and hospitable people who are always willing to share their cultural heritage and provide insight on familiar 'haunts' and 'finds', which could be discovered off the beaten track. The Victoria Falls offers crystal blue water and excellent surfer's waves. Looking for a party? Then plan your trip during one of the city's many festivals. A number of luminaries from all over the country perform in Victoria Falls. Feeling adventurous? Explore the diverse terrain of Victoria Falls that offers a number of activities to enjoy, including bird watching. In Victoria Falls they mastered the art of fine living; there is a vibrant culture, passionate in sport, mainly golf and full of life. Very soon, Victoria Falls will boast of having an airport with the longest runway in the world!' It was therefore not surprising that when the students arrived at Victoria Falls, they already had high expectations based on the chief's colourful explanation.

These are some of the diverse activities the students would eventually experience when they reached their fourth destination in the tour of Zimbabwe- the Victoria Falls. As the chief had explained, their visit confirmed without doubt that the Victoria Falls is one of the most spectacular of the seven natural wonders of the world. They gazed at the Mighty Zambezi as it flowed, broad and placid, to the brink of a basalt lip seventeen hundred meters wide before taking a headlong plunge into the frothy chasm of the gorge below. This is the world's largest sheet of falling water. Although its fame has spread far and wide, its natural surroundings have been left unspoilt. It was clear to them that the power of the Zambezi is undisputed. It is home to world famous rapids that vary in difficulty from novice to advanced. They watched white water rapids such as 'the devil's toilet', and 'stairway to heaven' sounds far more ominous than they seem from the water. The Zambezi boasts many grade 5 rapids, the highest level of rapid possible to attempt. The Zambezi River rises in

North West Zambia, from a spring in Kaloma and runs for 2750km. It is the 4th longest river in Africa and traverses 6 countries on its journey to the Indian Ocean. Victoria Falls Zimbabwe is dubbed as the best white water rafting experience in the world! The Zambezi River is classified as a high volume, pool-drop river. That means there is very little exposed rock either in the rapids or the pools below the rapids. The distance between rapids varies from 100m to two kilometres. The gorge itself is approximately 400ft deep at the put-in point, and 750ft at the take-out point. The river drops about 400ft over the 24km covered in the one-day raft trip, and the depth of the river can reach 200ft. Bungee Jumping 111 meters off the Victoria Falls Bridge has to be one of the most challenging, terrifying and crazy things to do.

The students were welcomed to this 'world of wonders' both for recreation and for a team building exercise. When their helicopter touched down cutting through a magnificent rainbow, some local children was already there singing with expectation while awaiting their arrival. The sky was blue with thin white clouds and there was a slight breeze but the weather was very warm. Mosi-o-Tunya looked magnificent. The sun was shining. It was a pleasantly warm day. The grass was tall and green, and the trees looked happy with red and soft leaves *(pfumvudza)*, which beautifully adorned the forest like a bride, whilst the wild animals grazed with poise and grace. Various birds of the forest were flying and chatting in the skies as if they were having a big party up on high.

The children were singing the song '*Shiri yakanaka unoendepei. Huya huya tifare. Kuti tifanane nemakore*' and '*Mvura naya naya tidye mupunga, Mvura naya naya tidye mupunga*'. They welcomed their visitors and gave them spring water served in traditional gourds. 'The students immediately joined the furore, and as soon as they caught the basic words of the song, also sang alongside the local children as they made their way to the waterfall through the tree groves that had different kinds of birds and animal species.

After the singing session, the students were treated to a buffet of African cuisine, with drinks served the traditional way under grass-thatched gazebos. In the background, the song Mosi-o - Tunya was playing continuously adding to the magic of the moment. After the buffet, they were given time to relax. Some of the students went to take a nap to re-charge their batteries before the afternoon training session began.

The first part of that afternoon's session was led by Troy, whose father is a well-known actor and pilot. He was chosen to lead the session because he had managed to successfully lead his team to come first when they competed in both the white water rafting, and bungee jumping sessions, by using the techniques he had learnt from his father. The other young people asked him some specific questions on how one's positive attitude is necessary in achieving dreams. The first question came from Tanaka, a head girl at her school in the town of Chinhoyi.

'Troy, to be honest I was amazed at how you led your team during the rafting event, and how you also managed to do such a huge leap from the bridge into the water when you bungee jumped. Please can you tell us where you got such skills from?'

'You know what Taneka, Tanaka, I mean, is that the right way to pronounce your name please? I am sure all of us are equally capable of doing what I did. Yes you might say I am talented but I don't think I was born talented. Here is my trick, if I can call it that. From an early age, my parents taught me to value an 'I can do it' attitude. I remember one day, my dad sat me down after our basketball team had been thrashed badly in College tournaments in Michigan. After the game, I was very frustrated and ended up kicking the ball into the crowd and threw a tantrum as I left the court.

'My father sat me down and said to me, 'Son, in life, your attitude can take you down the drain or up to the top of the mountain. You might be very talented but if your attitude is not right, you will not be able to achieve your dreams. The way you view the world, others, setbacks, success and yourself, might, in some circumstances, matter more than your talent'.

'From that day, I made a choice that I would view the world and others positively. When I succeed, I celebrate, but if I fail, I know that isn't the end of the world. Instead of blaming everybody, I sit down and reflect on where I went wrong, and how circumstances might have let me down. Thereafter, I dust myself up and make a plan on how I can improve where I need to improve, and how I can work around those things that I can't change. For example, when I was paddling today, I noticed that we couldn't change the high water waves but instead of sitting and complaining, we took advantage of the rough waves to propel our boat forward. At the same time, I led my team by example as I paddled the hardest while I also encouraged them to do the same.

'You see, my attitude didn't just come to me naturally, but my parents raised me in an environment that valued positive attitudes. I also had to make a choice to learn from their attitude. My early life at home helped me a great deal in shaping the person that I am today. My parents always told me, 'Son you can do it' and, therefore, I believed that I could. The training encouraged me to wake up early for my basketball practice before everyone else was up. By the time everyone was up, I made sure my bed was already sorted and went to bath without my parents' prompting. By the time I was ten, I could do pretty much everything from my homework, tidying up and making my own breakfast. It was those small disciplines at home that I simply adopted in every other area of my life. Coming from a home like that, it was not surprising that I did not get discouraged by peer negative pressure because I had a winning mentality ingrained in me. I go out into the world with a mentality to win, and the world has no choice but to help me win. At home whenever we are tempted to be complacent and acquiescing to the status quo, our dad often creates tensions that make us uncomfortable and motivate us to move on towards our goals. We are, therefore, constantly on the move, creating waves as I did today, coping well with change. When we think it's time to rest on our laurels, our dad coaches us to destroy the laurels. For example, he often takes us to our second home in Barbados to ride on the waves in the sea. This has helped us to ride on the waves of life towards our goals when others are running away from them. Where others see danger, we see opportunities.

'I know that it's not all of us who come from privileged homes where they are set up to succeed. However, that doesn't mean that we can't adopt correct attitudes if we grew up in difficult circumstances. Although people and circumstances can take away everything from you, what they can't take away is your attitude, because it lives right within you in the form of the small choices you make every day. For example, here in Africa, where you have very strong communities, if you come from a less privileged family, instead of giving up or resorting to life on the streets, you can approach the village head or your teacher for help. The extended family is also there to help you with options. Some of us from the developed world don't have access to these privileges at all. If your immediate family lets you down, the next place you find yourself is in a care home, which is not an ideal option at all.

'What is wrong with Care Homes?' asked Ndombo.

'Well, it would take me a day to tell you what is wrong with Care Homes, but believe you me, there is no way the government could effectively play the role that your parents and the extended family plays in your life. The care system in the West simply doesn't work. If it worked, children who are taken into care would all be doing well, but that isn't the case right now, and things appear to be getting worse.'

'Troy, you spoke about choices, but are one's choices different from one's beliefs?' Farai asked.

'Not exactly, but the two are related. Your beliefs normally develop from the way you think although the way you think can also be shaped up by the environment in which you live. For example, you may come from a family where nobody has ever passed their 'A' levels, and you in turn grow up with a belief that you would never pass such exams. In such instances, you have a choice whether to believe that falsehood or to tell yourself that you can be the first one to pass and go to university. Sometimes you need to look beyond your immediate family and tell yourself 'if so and so could pass, why can't I too?' In other words, there are times when you have to look for role models outside your family, especially if your family has negative attitudes that create a toxic environment. However, that doesn't mean that you should not respect your family. You can still continue to learn from them in some respects, but also learn from others regarding issues that they aren't good at. It's wrong to disown your parents for the reason that they aren't that successful. You should continue to respect them, listen to them, and involve them in major decisions concerning your life.

'You should always have confidence that you will achieve your dreams. One of the greatest Americans, Walt Disney, once said, '*the secret of making dreams come true can be summarized in four C's. They are Curiosity,*

Confidence, Courage, and Constancy; and the greatest of these is Confidence'. Although confidence on its own can't fully compensate for other life circumstances, for instance poverty, an attitude of confidence can enable you to venture into the world beyond your immediate environment in pursuit of opportunities. Just look at the founding fathers of America, for example, through confidence, they left their comfortable lives in Europe in search of better opportunities in the jungles. What I am saying might sound very detached from your world, but attitude matters in our daily lives. For example, some of you might be thinking of going abroad to further your studies. On the other hand some of us from abroad might be thinking of coming to live in Africa, volunteering in various projects and exploring various money-making opportunities. You may not even know where to begin but the right attitude can enable you to overcome discouragement as you hunt for opportunities. You might find yourself making several telephone calls or making many applications for a job, but with very minimal results to show for your effort. However, the day you give up might be the day you were about to land on an opportunity. You have to keep on trying in the face of discouragement.

'An attitude of perseverance is not acquired overnight but comes as a result of your ability to begin, and complete small daily tasks. For example, your mum might sign you for swimming lessons, and when you begin, you might be very enthusiastic until you find out that it's not that easy to swim like a fish. If you quickly give up, it means that next time when you are faced with an equally difficult task, for example in the work place, you might easily give up.'

While Troy was speaking, one of the students posed a question, 'What if I find out that swimming isn't my hobby?'

Troy continued, 'Well it's not so much a question whether swimming is your hobby or not. The issue is more to do with having a finisher's mentality.

'In the job market today or even when you apply for a university place, they are likely to ask you to tell them about a task that you began and successfully completed, because they know that quite a lot of students waste public money by taking up university places and then dropping out when faced with the first hurdle. It is, therefore, crucial that we get our attitudes right from the word go by disciplining our thinking and daily habits, because the discipline we get from daily thoughts and habits will in turn determine our thoughts and decisions when it really counts in life. It is like a cycle because negative thoughts give rise to negative beliefs, and negative beliefs lead to wrong decisions, which in turn lead to wrong actions and continual bad actions lead to bad habits, then negative thoughts and the cycle begins again. I sincerely believe that with the right attitude, we may not all be able to jump like I did earlier today or be pilots and actors like my dad, but I am sure that we can achieve our own respective dreams. We can overcome discouragement; we can face fear and do it anyway in the face of that fear. We can use our failure to gain a new perspective and move on, and above all we can also help our peers to do them same. Thank you.'

When Troy finished his 'Question and Answer' session on attitude, there was a huge round of applause. All the students were fired up to do something about their attitudes. They were talking about having diaries in which they would record their major decisions on attitude and some were talking of starting peer accountability circles of support. Others were talking about finding a community or school mentor. Ndombo was confident that Chief Nehoreka would be her right mentor. That's how excited the students were about how one's attitude could largely determine how far one would go in life in achieving their dreams. That evening they actually needed time to reflect on this issue as a way of taking stock on where they were with regard to attitude, and thinking on how best to move forward when they began university in the fall. It had been emphasized to them that the training sessions would ideally be followed by reflection and planning, otherwise they would lose all they had learnt in the heat of the moment and excitement. All the students had to get diaries to jot down their thoughts and plan ahead. They spent the remaining two days at Victoria Falls having all forms of training in aquatic sports and fishing, while at the same time having a lot of fun.

Chapter 5: Great Zimbabwe Masvingo

BEFORE their helicopter entered the VaKaranga airspace, Chief Nehoreka explained to them how he had been raised there in a village close to the city of Masvingo. He explained how his current village in Chimanimani replicated some of his ancestors' habits and customs. He had told them how his generation had been raised in the early 20th century. He continued, 'I was born and bred in a closely-knit community where my father was a Murozvi chief who led a clan that made the first ever attempt to go to the moon without a space shuttle! Apart from my stint at Kutama College where I was educated under the watchful Jesuits pious eyes and another overseas stint during the liberation war, Masvingo was always my home whilst growing up until we moved to Chimanimani. Our homestead was in the centre of the village, just like most Shona villages. Our dwellings were expertly designed out of granite rock, being the parent rock of the region. The homestead was built by my father's most experienced architects using a method called dry-stone walling, demanding a high level of expertise in masonry. Some of the site is built on natural rock formations. The perimeter structure comprised a huge enclosing wall some 20 metres high. Inside there are concentric passageways, along with a number of enclosures. One of these was the royal enclosure. Large quantities of gold and ceremonial battle-axes, along with other objects were also stored there. It was always thought that the village was built on huge deposits of diamonds.

'My father kept an old drum with an uncharacteristic burnt-black bottom hole called a *ngoma*. This ngoma was a combination of reliquary, drum and primitive weapon, fueled with a somewhat unpredictable proto-gunpowder. Through this *ngoma*, my father was able to speak to God. Thus from an early age, I realised the importance of living in a natural environment that promoted good health and I also appreciate how we could all use faith as a tool in creating strong communities. Now more than ever, you are growing up in a world in which religion poses the greatest threat to human existence, but that shouldn't be the case. If properly understood and practised, religion can contribute to world peace. More so, peace-loving religious communities could be hedges of protection to people who are in need. This need might be in the form of spiritual poverty, which is why one of the Hebrew Scholars once said, *'Blessed are the poor in spirit because they shall inherit the kingdom of God'*. The sense of belonging and connection that religion can bring can be a protective factor against human primitive anxieties, which are the major causes of mental health problems in the developed world where most of you come from. I will be addressing this topic in one of our training sessions latter.'

As the Chief continued to speak passionately from an aerial view, the students could see the sprawling, yet intact, rock solid Great Zimbabwe Monument. The structure was intricately designed out of granite rock just as the Chief had said. When they alighted from the helicopter, expectant local young people and students came to welcome them. Each one was competing for an opportunity to hug and welcome the visitors to the province of Masvingo. The throng was shouting with excitement and someone called out, 'Troy, what's up man? Doug, Are you all right?' The level of hospitality overwhelmed the young students. Soft drinks and light food were served before they had a tour of Great Zimbabwe. They attended a series of workshops and discussions that covered various topics including the role of faith, mental well-being, how young people can contribute in creating a big society, green technology, and global warming.

A local student mentor called Jekanyika spoke at length on how one's social environment contributes to their life outcomes. He also spoke about the work he was doing with local youths from the time he recovered from mental illness. He told them that part of his work was to pay back to the community that had supported him during his recovery process.

He continued, 'We work with young people who have been affected by negative changes in their lives. We equip them with the skills and tools to deal with change, for example, rejection and family deaths. Last week we were working with a group of teens who lost their parents and one of the things that we emphasized to them was that one's perception of an event or experience powerfully affects their emotional, behavioural and physiological responses to it.

'We pair these teens with a circle of support to ensure that the people around them and other resources become a protective factor that alloys them from pain. We have managed to enlist the support of wealthy people in our nation to give these young people life chances. For example, some business people have been donating money and clothes to ensure that we improve the course and outcome of these children's lives. Some wealthy people who run safaris have offered them holidays for rest and respite.

'We are making attempts to roll out this programme right across the country to ensure that no child is left behind because every child matters. That's the reason why we have chosen this place, The Great Zimbabwe, as the venue for our meeting this year. That is why we have chosen the theme for this year's workshops as *Building Big and Bold People.* After days of prayer and fasting, we felt that God impressed on our heart that this is the direction our country needs to take. We chose the books of Ezra and Nehemiah to be our guiding scriptures for this year's conference. These books are relevant at a time when we are all trying to build and patch up so that Zimbabwe could become a great Zimbabwe once again.

'Just like Zimbabwe, the nation of Israel was in a similar position of political crisis at the end of the Babylonian captivity. Although Zimbabweans are not exactly in captivity, there are lessons that could be drawn from the Jewish experience in seeking direction in these trying times. When some of the Jews who had gone into captivity were about to return, God raised

Ezra and Nehemiah. Ezra had an effective ministry in teaching the law, initiating reforms, and in guiding people in rebuilding the Hebrew theocracy upon which God's relationship with his people would sit and take strength. On the other hand, Nehemiah was an expert builder, great reformer, and was experienced in policy-making and implementation. He didn't only help in building the walls of Jerusalem, but in building big people with big hearts for each other.'

After Jekanyika's speech, the students had an opportunity to do some group activities and group presentations to display their talents and teamwork. Doug's group did the most fascinating presentations. Doug had been put in the same group with about ten local youths who were involved in various technical subjects in their schools and colleges. They titled their project 'Envision', and agreed to come up with a model house, which could be replicated in reality, to enable citizens to be housed in decent but cheap accommodation. They first sketched the model house on a canvass. After this, they built a makeshift version of it in front of all present, using bits of material they had picked from the surroundings. Since the local boys were very polite, they asked their guest, Doug, to draw the sketch. Doug did not need to do a lot of thinking. He quickly sketched a house that had a foundation of stones, which resembled the Great Zimbabwe Monument. Above the ground it looked very modern and was made out of environmentally friendly material. In a real life situation electricity would be generated by the wind. The contraption looked very simple and was African in outlook. Doug's group quickly and easily assembled the house in front of the large group. This eco-friendly, makeshift house, allowed natural light to come into it and the thatch was done in such a way that it would capture rainwater for recycling. All the young people present were amazed. They thought Doug would model his design on the houses he had seen in London, but he confounded them by his understanding of local culture and how this could be harmonized with environmentally friendly technology.

When he was asked to explain the concept behind this makeshift house, he told them that Africa was full of natural resources, but there was a danger that its resources were being used to construct structures that looked western in style at the expense of being environmentally friendly. He emphasized that Zimbabweans needed to harmonize local knowledge, local resources, and latest research, in coming up with affordable and sustainable housing for all in the same way Habitat for Humanity did across the world. He said it was very important for young Design students to research into products that were friendly to the environment.

'Development must be rooted in local values, which is why I have put foundations of stone that represent Great Zimbabwe. However, having local values is only the starting point, because we don't live in the past. We cannot keep on living in the caves and neither should we keep on looking back at yesterday's achievements at the expense of what matters today and tomorrow, because today matters too. When you build your country, please look back to get strength from what your fathers did. For example, they left a very good country teeming with natural resources for you. They also liberated it and gave you an identity. You need to preserve all that history, and let it be a basis for you to build a strong, prosperous, sustainable and vibrant society. If you keep on looking back, but without meeting today's demands and tomorrow's challenges, you may do so at the expense of other discoveries that God has in store for you. That is why the house I have drawn has modern architecture above the ground but with an ancient underground foundation. Everything in life requires balance. You have such a beautiful country and if you get the balance right I have no doubt that the new Zimbabwe will be much brighter than the old Zimbabwe although both have a pivotal role to play in your history. Thank you.'

There was a resounding applause for Doug. Next day the local newspapers carried the story.

***

When Doug went to bed that day it took him quite some time to fall asleep. He mused over many things, but one thing that kept coming to his mind was the group of black Zimbabwean men dressed like Jews, who the chief had invited to attend that day's workshops. The chief had kept referring to them as friends. They had snow-white hair and beards because of old age. They all had Jewish skullcaps. One of them was said to be a powerful Karanga Chief. Although Doug had been raised in an English family, he had been told by his father that his paternal ancestors were Jewish. His surname, Cohen, was actually Jewish and not English. His father had once told him that their ancestors had migrated to Europe way back in the past centuries. There was no denying that Jewish blood ran through Doug's family. This had led Doug to embark on a heritage search that he did without his father's knowledge. Many times he would disappear to Golders Green and Stamford Hill just to feed his curiosity about his origins.

The trappings of English modernity, the middle class talk of ping-pong balls, and concertos had severed his umbilical cord from the land of Promise that God had sworn to Abraham, his patriarch. Doug's father was an avowed atheist and one of the leading British astronauts. He had worked on many projects including the Beagle, which was sent into space before it just disappeared in 2003. It was very hard for Doug to reconcile his Jewish tradition with the English environment of concertos, paintings, and astrophysics that his father had exposed him to, although he always tried to. When he saw the 'black Jews', he was prompted to reflect on the enormity of his culture's impact on other world cultures.

He fell asleep while pondering on the events of the day. He was not asleep for long before he woke up from a dream that made him restless. In the dream, he saw a procession of people who were walking from a place that was called Jerusalem. They were fair-skinned like most Jews, and wore long beards like Jesus' disciples did. They had camels loaded with food and other items, a flock of sheep and goats in front of them. His father was also there carrying him (Doug) on the back. When he asked his father where they were going, his father told him that they were fleeing from a tribal war, but didn't disclose where they were going. What also surprised him was the presence of black Jewish people among them. In the dream, when the procession reached a certain desert, twelve white-robed men had a meeting and agreed that they were going to part ways. Some decided to camp there in the desert. Others went to a place called Europa, but one black man who looked like the man Doug had seen earlier at the work-shop, decided to go to a place called Kush. The most confusing aspect of the dream was the mixture of modern day people and some ancient people whose language had a paucity of syllables because of their limited and under-developed language skills.

When the black man decided to go to Kush (Africa), some of his brothers tried to dissuade him from the idea, telling him that it was very dangerous to venture into a continent, which, beyond Egypt and Ethiopia, the tribe of Israel knew nothing about. The rest of the men asked him angrily 'Are you serious that you want to take a leap of faith into the unknown Dark Continent?' His brother, Simeon, asked him with a deep sense of concern.

The Black Jew looked his brother in the eye and said, 'Have you forgotten the promise? Have you forgotten the covenant, my brother?'

When Simeon remained concerned about the safety of his brother together with his family, the Black Jew began to explain to his brother that it was essential to take that step of faith and to follow his heart. He quoted the story of their father Abraham.

'Our heritage and spiritual legacy was set by our father Abraham, who believed in the promise, and set out to go to Canaan without questioning why God wanted him to go there. His was an act of faith which was why God called him his friend. Our father always followed on his commitments. When God called him to a distant land, he went the distance. Our father Abraham did not doubt the promise. He did not doubt the vision that he would possess all the land that he set his foot on. Did he question God? No! He took a leap of faith into the unknown. In life one has to learn to follow their heart, take risks, make mistakes and never regret. There is a path that is laid out before every one of us, but you have to find that path. In life it is those who dare to win who eventually win. I have every confidence that I will be successful in Kush. I will be able to leave a Jewish legacy wherever I set my feet'.

When Doug woke up from the dream, he had more questions than answers. Although he felt restless, he felt an amazing ripple of peace within him. However, he still required some answers to some of the questions he had. He woke up and asked one of the guards at the compound to go and call Chief Nehoreka because he wanted to ask him something urgent. When the guard went to wake up the chief, he realised that the Chief hadn't slept but was sorting out the following day's schedule. The chief rushed to Doug's room fearing that something might have gone wrong, but when he entered the room, Doug looked quite relaxed.

'Sorry Chief for waking you up after such an eventful day,' Doug said, as he looked at Chief Nehoreka who, despite his advanced age, looked very strong and alert. He assured Doug that it was okay to wake him up.

'I hadn't slept as yet, but was sorting out our schedule for tomorrow. I go to bed at 12 midnight and ensure that I have seven hours of sleep.'

'Wow, that's an amazing life for someone your age,' Doug replied looking impressed.

The chief responded while he made himself comfortable.

'You know what son? Age is in the mind, and old age does not mean one stops to have dreams and goals. The day one ceases to be excited about their future is the day one stops living. Many people stop living very early in life but I have chosen to keep on living until I die.' Doug was very impressed.

The chief continued, 'Well, I have been informed that you have something profound to share with me. How may I help you, please?' Doug didn't quite know where to begin but after summoning courage and regaining his composure, he began to talk.

'When we arrived here earlier I was surprised to see men who looked Jewish. You see, my dad once told me that we are Jewish although we have lived like English people in all respects. So if I am a British Jew, are there some Zimbabwean black Jews as well?'

'Before I respond, may I have the permission to call Samuel, please?' The chief asked.

'Who is Samuel?' Doug asked curiously.

83

'Samuel is one of the chiefs who lives locally, but who has ties with the Jews.' The chief went out and quickly brought Chief Samuel Mutero. As soon as Doug saw him, he saw the resemblance with the man he had seen in his dream, but didn't want to quickly make a comment.

'I will let Samuel explain everything to you as he has personal knowledge about the Jews.'

Chief Samuel spoke about his origins from the Lemba tribe, which settled in Southern Africa several hundreds of years back. When the chief posed, Doug reflected on the dream that he had just had, and encouraged Chief Mutero to carry on with his explanation. The chief continued.

'Our tribe can be traced back to Jacob and Abraham. We have always followed religious traditions that share many similarities with those of the Jews. Though we speak a Bantu language, some of our traditions vary greatly from those of other Bantu people. We came from the north, from a place called Senna. We left Senna, crossed Pusela, came to Africa, and there we rebuilt Senna.'

Doug was listening pensively and nodding his head as Chief Samuel Mutero narrated how his ancestors settled in Masvingo, and how they brought with them the remains of the Jewish Ark of the Covenant.

'We brought our traditions here. However, we now believe that because the world is now a global village, we are now global citizens. We have since learnt the Bantu traditions for centuries but we also still hold on to some of our ancestral practices. It is essential to learn from others in order to expand your world view.'

'So in a way, I am related to you then?' Doug enquired curiously.

'In fact, all human beings are related. We are all members of the human family which is why it is essential to live and work together in harmony,' the chief responded, spreading his arms around to emphasize his point.

'It must have been a terrible journey then,' Doug suggested.

'Which journey?' Asked Chief Samuel.

'I mean the journey that you took from the Middle East, because I saw you in my dream, coming from the Middle East. I had a dream in which you were with your brothers in the Middle East. They were discouraging you from coming to Africa, but you told them that God wanted you to come to Africa,' Doug related his dream to Chief Samuel Mutero.

The Chief paused in reflection as he recollected the history of the Jewish people from the books he had read, particularly the book of Maccabees.

'If you saw a person like me in your dream, it must have been my ancestor because their journey from there happened centuries ago, way before I was born. May be God just wanted to reveal something to you. From the records I have, they say it was a very treacherous journey. They had to cross some seas, mountains and rivers with crocodiles and some of them died on the way.' The chief told Doug.

'But why did they do that, risking their lives?' Doug asked, his mouth agape.

The chief immediately responded, 'It was the promise. It had to be done. They had to fulfil the prophecy, and God's will for the Jews. It is not only the Jews who are born with a promise. Every human being is. When we are born we all hold a promise in our clenched fist. Locked in the promise are talents and gifts that help you to achieve the promise. The gifts unlock the promise but you have to use them in order for this to happen. It's a tragedy that many people grow old and die without having realised their promises. Some hold on to the promise but some lose it due to life's circumstances. I am sure you have come here to reclaim your promise. You have come to reclaim a part of your heritage. When you leave this place your life will never be the same again. I like your humility and eagerness to learn. Humility and an open mind are the starting points in self-discovery and personal growth. I also like your curiosity. It comes from your intuition because we all want to know where we came from, and what promise we were given by God when we were born. On a philosophical level, that's the fundamental question for all human beings. When you are not in touch with your roots, you feel as if you have lost touch with the world. We carry the past with us as if it has just happened. It gives us grounding.

'As you mature, in order to succeed and fully enjoy your life, you need to know yourself (identity), what you are capable of achieving (your potential), where you are coming from (your heritage), why you were born (your purpose), and where you are going (your destiny). I am glad that today you have discovered your destiny, and from today you will begin to discover the other four facets that will anchor you when life's storms rage, and winds of adversity threaten to uproot you. You will find your promise as you continue your inner search. From your restlessness, I can see that you have already begun the search.'

'What did the Shona tribes who lived here think when the Jewish people pitched up overnight wearing long clothes and carrying an Ark of the Covenant?' Doug asked again, imagine the curiosity of the local people when they saw the strangers.

The chief responded thoughtfully. 'Well, I am sure there was a bit of panic, although my ancestors were welcomed by the Shonas. When they came, the Varozvi tribe was busy trying to figure out how they could build the Great Zimbabwe walls that surround this compound. They welcomed my ancestors and gave them land. Since then our cultures have been intertwined. For example, we use stonework in building our houses, which some of the locals have since adopted in building walls and caves where they used to bury their dead. Look at Khami ruins for example! In addition, my Jewish ancestors had prophets and used the Ark of the Covenant to reach out to God. Quite a number of Zimbabweans also use the spirit medium and the drum (ngoma) as a way of reaching out to God in their traditional worship. We might never get to fully know the extent to which Jewish culture influenced Zimbabwean culture, but all I can tell you is that there is no doubt that most of them are now also heirs to the promise of Abraham. I have come across a lot of them who live by faith, who rejoice at justice. The just shall live by faith'.

Still talking, the chief took Doug outside into the tropical night. He asked him to look up into the sky and at the horizon. 'What do you see, and how do you feel?' The chief enquired.

'I feel peace and I see galaxies and galaxies of stars.'

With a curious swing of the arm, the chief made motions around Doug's abdomen with his open palm as if he was imparting something.

'Receive your promise today, peace shall be your portion, and just like your ancestor Abraham, great is your inheritance.'

Doug fell to the ground in a trance and began worshipping God. The following morning, he built an altar and called it 'peace'. As he dedicated the altar to his God the following morning in the presence of other students and the village chiefs, he uttered solemnly, 'Great shall be Zimbabwe, and great shall be the peace and prosperity within her borders.' He told the chiefs that his nation and the nation of Zimbabwe were bound by cords of love that could not be broken, and that they were bound together by a shared history, values and friendship. It was at Great Zimbabwe that Doug learnt that greatness is within every one of us, but that it is up to you to search for it and find it. There is a hero and an answer right inside, but that hero has to be sought out and the answer ought to be retrieved.

Chapter 8: Chinhoyi

IT was a sunny day in the village. The villagers were at *Gogo* Ndoro's homestead helping her to harvest her maize and peanuts. They all looked hopeful and energized under the searing heat of the African sun. There was something in the African sun that gave them hope and courage even in the face of discouragement. Its shining every morning announced the arrival of another day, brought with it a sense of renewal and revitalization. The unfailing sun told them that if you did not succeed yesterday, today- a new day, another day, you could always try again to reach for the stars. That is exactly what they were all doing there, everyday, when the African sun rose. They did without questioning that which had to be done, and whose time was due: tilling the land, harvesting their crops, filling their barns and serving each other whole-heartedly as a closely-knit community. The economic difficulties outside the village did not affect their daily routines that much.

Such was the order of the day when the students arrived in this village, located near the Chinhoyi Caves where *Gogo* Ndoro hosted them for a 'Cultural Exposure and Exchange Tour' as *Gogo* chose to call it. Since *Gogo* lived right in the countryside, the students left their helicopter in Chinhoyi town and were ferried by ox-drawn scotch-carts to *Gogo*'s homestead. Being on a scotch cart was such a steep learning experience for most of these students. As they passed through the forests along the Lomagundi road, it wasn't unusual to see small animals and reptiles retreating into the thickets, fleeing the noise from oxen hooves and the squeaking cartwheels. Everywhere birds were singing and chirping in the woods. As they drew closer and closer to the village, Doug heard a bird which went, 'Tweet, tweet, and tweet', and he alerted his friends to listen, as he thought it was referring to a social networking site called Twitter. The bird kept on making this sound flying right in front of the cart from tree top to tree top until it perched on *Gogo's* mulberry tree, which was laden with ripe mulberries.

The carts eventually arrived at *Gogo's* homestead. Doug and the others saw that there was a welcome party already in place. *Gogo* Ndoro, some villagers and children from the local school, stood waiting for the visitors to disembark from the scorch-cart. They were all there to help *Gogo*, and to extend hospitality to the visiting students from faraway lands. The school children rushed forward in one wave, eager to welcome their visitors. A few hardy dogs with wagging tails, erect ears and tails, stood barking uncertainly. There was a great deal of mayhem and excitement. Hens took off into the air like Concorde jets while at the same time a puff of dust rose from all these activities, and ascended into the air. 'Welcome *vazukuru*. You are all my grandsons and granddaughters. Welcome Americans, and welcome Britons! How are you?' *Gogo* Ndoro said with excitement as she wiped her wet palms on her blue apron before she greeted each one of the students with a traditional handshake. The cart was parked on the cart-pad. As the students alighted from the carts onto a raised earthen platform, *Gogo*

90

cautioned them to mind the gap between the cart and the platform edge.

'Give them water and water melons, and make sure they sit comfortably', *Gogo* Ndoro instructed the younger villagers whom she also called her granddaughters and grandsons. Every young person coming to see her was either a grandson or a granddaughter.

The students settled, with the boys sitting on wooden Tonga stools and benches, whilst the girls sat on expensive goat-skin mats. *Gogo* Ndoro began talking, 'We welcome you all to our village. I have no doubt that you will learn so much from our culture and traditions as we also seek to learn from yours. You see, the world has become like a village. It is, therefore, very important that we understand the world and the different cultures in it in order for us to do business effectively with each other. For example, here I grow cotton and other produce that are sold to Western countries and the Far East; therefore, it has become necessary for me to read journals on international trade and understand the cultural dynamics that impact on trade. I would like you to feel free my grand sons and daughters. Please ask any questions you want to. I grant you the liberty of this village. This is your home. We are all related as members of the human family.'

Kirsty asked, 'Are all these people here members of your family because you keep on calling them your grandsons and daughters and we also notice that they are working for you?' *Gogo* Ndoro replied, 'No, Kesiti (Kirsty), here in Zimbabwe it is our culture that you treat your neighbour as if you are related to them by blood.

We are all a family. If I travel, for example, my neighbour can take care of my children without asking for any payment.'

'Is that allowed by Social Services then?' Laura asked. *Gogo* Ndoro was amused, and she giggled before she responded.

'We have no such thing as social services running our families here in Africa. We are free and we aren't as paranoid as westerners like you tend to be. I understand that your government in Britain is talking about creating a big society. Let me assure you, if people just love each other in the same way they love themselves, the government wouldn't be bothered about creating a big society, but the big society would organically create itself. You cannot force people to love each other. They have to make a choice to do so. I am also aware that your government back home is proposing to measure people's well being through a happiness index. Those are very noble ideas, but please go and tell them that *Gogo* said love is the key to happiness. If you all learn to love one another despite your racial differences, your society will indeed be a very happy one no matter what the weather might be like. '

'How about these children who are working in your barns, isn't that child labour? Do you pay them at all?' One of the Canadian students asked.

Gogo Ndoro smiled and cleared her throat before she responded, 'No *muzukuru*, in Africa we have what we call *ubuntu*. *Ubuntu* is at the heart of our communities and society. We might not have a perfect political leadership, which is the case in every country, but our societies work very well. Our communities are strong and cohesive although things are beginning to change because our children are emigrating abroad and when they come back, they barely recognize the extended family as their relatives, let alone other villagers. I will not spend much time talking about this now, because this evening we will discuss this issue around a bonfire to get your views on this. In the mean time, please enjoy the weather and go around the village or back to Chinhoyi town to view our local scenery. You can follow the village loop to the Chinhoyi Caves. I always jog along that loop every morning. A few hundred meters from here, please turn left and then right and go round the mountain range for 45 degrees. Stop right there. You will meet Nicodemus' sons. Ask them to accompany you around the mountain range just in case you encounter scary animals of the forest.'

The students got into groups with the village children and immediately began conversing together like long-lost relatives. They walked together in small groups past *Sekuru* Samson's homestead where they stopped briefly to chat to him and to watch him working with an adze on his crafts. He was putting the finishing touches to a pair of ox yokes. From there their next port of call was the Apostle's house. The apostolic man had a shaven head and a beard like that of American rapper Rick Ross. He was busy making some water containers using wrought iron whilst humming a song that repeated the words 'Hosanna'.

'Is he a rap artist?' Troy asked. One of the village boys called Tawanda told him that the man wasn't a rap artist, but a sect member praising his God through song. He told him that the man belonged to an indigenous apostolic sect in the village.

Their walk took them to more places where they met all sorts of people and saw many interesting things. The whole scene had the feel of a surrealistic oil painting on canvas: hens clucking and wandering in the nearby bushes, children herding cattle, women doing crotchet and embroidery work at a local cooperative event, and the inevitable drunken men engaging in a hilarious dance called *Borrowdale,* at a bottle store (pub).

Doug stopped by to work with women who were working on a project they called 'Tapestry of Hope'. They were weaving a portrait using various colours that represented Zimbabwe's diversity. They used very beautiful and diverse colours, illustrating overflowing rivers, beautiful people at work, green fields, and people who were holding each other by the waist as a sign of filial bonds. *Gogo* Ndoro liked the piece so much that she promised the group she would send it for display at the Harare International Festival of the Arts. *Gogo* believed in the intrinsic beauty of Zimbabwean art, especially when it portrayed its people who have rich values.

After marvelling at the women's piece they walked along the loop until they arrived at the Orange Grove Motel where they treated themselves to some fruit, after which they had a brief swimming session just to cool themselves from the searing heat.

After swimming they made their way to the Chinhoyi Caves- a network of mysterious and extensive caves composed of limestone and dolomite. The descent to the main cave comes suddenly upon a pool of impressive cobalt blue water. This pool is popularly called the Sleeping Pool or *Chirorodzira* (Pool of the Fallen), and is very ideal for keen divers. A few frogmen surfaced from the pool while Laura and the others watched in silent wonder, as they tried to assimilate the aura of the place.

Troy wanted to test his diving skills but got a little bit scared when one of the local boys told him that there were some magical mermaids in the water. In fact that wasn't actually the reason that dissuaded Troy, but the fact that he was very tired, and also didn't have the right diving equipment and clothing. One of the local girls- a Head Girl at a local school, explained to the visiting students that the caves were an important heritage site in Zimbabwe, and that they used to be an old refuge of Chief Chinhoyi during tribal wars a century earlier. She also explained how the Zimbabwe War of Liberation began in Chinhoyi, and how this had placed Chinhoyi on the map. In addition, she told them that the Zimbabwe president's countryside home was quite close to Chinhoyi.

'If you follow the President Robert Mugabe Highway, you will be at Mr Mugabe's place', the girl said.

'That sounds like President George Bush Turnpike highway in Texas!' Troy quipped.

The girl continued, 'Near his home is the famous Kutama College, where the president attended school together Chief Nehoreka, before they went abroad.'

As they stood near the edge of the pool, at the bottom of the cave, with the cobalt blue water as still as always, the young people felt bound together by cords of love that no person could ever break. They were like brothers and sisters in a new and binding faith that seemed to have something to do with the mystic aura of the caves. Silent voices told them that one day the world would be a better place; safe for all the children of the world to live and grow up in. It was not surprising that in that moment of awe and inspiration, one of the English boys, a huge fan of the British band 'Take That' began to sing a Take That song 'The Flood', while those who knew it joined in. Their voices echoed around the caves and had a subterranean ring. Part of the song went as follows:

Standing, on the edge of forever, At the start of whatever, Shouting love at the world. Back then, we were like cavemen, We'd beam at the moon and the stars. Then we forgave them....

It was amazing how, despite not having heard the song before, the local boys and girls were swept by its lyrics and melody and ended up joining in the singing. This confirmed the belief that music is as old as human beings. Our ancestors, who travelled from cave to cave, couldn't carry many things, but modern archaeology shows that, as well as the little they might have had with them in the way of food, there was always a musical instrument in their baggage, usually a drum. Music isn't just something that comforts or distracts us, it goes beyond that. It's an ideology. You can judge people by the kind of music they listen to. Music has the power to unite people, for example, look at how it unites people from diverse backgrounds at Glastonbury, Doug reflected quietly.

***

As the gracious African sun was beginning to set, the Head Girl told them that it was time to go back to the village. One of the visitors asked what time it was, to which she replied 'six o'clock', without even looking at her watch.

'How did you know it was six o'clock?' asked Laura.

'Here in Southern Africa when the sun is setting we know that it's six o'clock. We can also tell by the position and length of the shadows.' The visitors were fascinated by how significant the sun was in Africa. It appeared as though people's lives revolved around it. As the sun gradually sank, it gave way to the moon and the stars, marking the end of yet another day, and the start of yet another evening in the tropics.

On their way back to the village, they bought cheeseburgers from a snack shop at a petrol station. They ate the burgers as they walked into the encroaching darkness. They walked briskly along narrow paths, swamps and meadows. The noise made by their footsteps and the rustling of the grass on either side of the path woke up small creatures that were beginning to close their eyes to sleep.

On approaching the village they met several people, some who were coming from water wells while others were putting the cattle in their pens for the night.. Troy and a few others helped a boy who was having problems driving his herd of cattle into the pen. After that, they passed through a homestead that appeared deserted. The thatch on the huts was beginning to fall off and the courtyard was overgrown with weeds. When they passed through, they felt a hair-raising silence and a sense of discomfort until a barking dog that looked lost and hungry interrupted the silence. Doug wanted to rescue the dog but was strongly advised not to by one of the local boys. When he asked why he couldn't help a poor dog, the local boy told him that this was a haunted homestead. The old couple that had once lived there had since died, but before they died, they were very unpopular. They were revered village witches. The heavy atmosphere in the homestead was caused by their restless spirits that continued to reside there long after they had died. They owned the barking dog that had since taken habitation in the wilderness and was now called a wild dog. Occasionally the wild dog came back to the homestead. It was as if some unseen force drove it back to its former haunts. It was, therefore, advisable to leave that dog alone.

'Didn't the couple have any children at all who could take over this piece of land?' Doug enquired further.

'They had a daughter called Evelyn. When her first husband died ten years ago, she went to England and where we heard that she re-married and is now called Mrs. Peters. When she was recently in Zimbabwe, she didn't bother to visit Chinhoyi, but stayed in a lodge with her son Thomas,' the local boy replied as they proceeded to *Gogo's* place.

Back at *Gogo's* homestead, dinner was served to them around a big bonfire. There was a lot of food to choose from, ranging from cooked, dried hare meat in thick peanut butter sauce, thick rapoko porridge (dough), pumpkin leaves vegetables, roasted pumpkin seeds and nuts seasoned in salt, churned milk, and a variety of desserts ranging from water melons to cucumbers.

They spoke about anything and everything, from politics to student exchange programmes, school curriculum and international relations. Meanwhile, Troy, feeling that he had eaten more than what his stomach could take, was now feeling very sleepy. Apart from the burger that he had eaten on their way back to *Gogo's* homestead, he had also eaten a lot of wild beans (*nyemba*), meat, and drunk a lot of milk. The other students stayed awake engaging each other socially and tapping into *Gogo's* wisdom.

'*Gogo*, please how can I change the world? How can I help every poor child I meet to succeed, *Gogo* please?' Alicia Chan, the girl from Hong Kong, asked.

Gogo giggled as usual before she gave a carefully prepared response.

'That's a very noble ambition grandchild. You have to begin by changing your own world. Your own world is right within you. For example, a person who has a poor attitude cannot change the world. You have to focus on improving yourself first and then aspire to change the world. Otherwise it would be a case of the blind leading the blind. This is just an example. I am not saying you have a poor attitude. The world that you would improve comprises your own attitude, your thinking and behaviour. The first commandment is for you to love your neighbour in the way you want to be loved. You have to begin small, and change your own world beginning with people who are close to you and those you meet in your world. It is the small things that make a difference. For example, your commitment to come and visit our country and realise that there is a big society behind Zimbabwean politics, is indeed a positive step in changing the world. You see what politicians do? They make people believe that everyone in this country is interested in politics only. Ever since you came to Zimbabwe have you come across a politician? Have you been beaten up or harassed?'

The students unanimously answered 'No, *Gogo*,'.

Gogo continued. 'I am sure you haven't, because Zimbabwe is larger than its politics. The majority of its citizens' aspiration is to raise their children who will in turn help to transform their communities. It's not like a political entity in the way the Western media has portrayed it.'

Gogo asked them to get into pairs and discuss ways in which they could help change the world for the better. They were to discuss their viewpoints as a group while nibbling snacks of roasted groundnuts around the bon fire in the open air. While they were busy talking, a strange-looking animal came from the dark, but they couldn't identify what it was as they could only see its bright eyes. A few girls and boys were frightened and almost screamed, but *Gogo* assured them that it was safe and that nothing would happen. She said she had carried out a health and safety assessment to ensure that her grandchildren would be safe. It subsequently transpired that the animal was a harmless jackal that had been attracted by the wafting smell of roasted beef. When Farai screamed at it, it simply retreated back into the dark in the same way it had come, as Gogo's dogs chased it. Loud howling in the dark followed this. With the jackal drama out of the way, they resumed their discussion.

'So what do you all say is the best way to make this world a better place? Are there any takers please? I suggest we do a Round Robin starting with you Tanaka,' *Gogo* suggested.

'Well, I guess it all boils down to relating well to others really, *Gogo*. What do you think?' Tanaka suggested.

'Can someone elaborate on Tanaka's point please?' *Gogo* asked, trying to encourage participation.

Ndombo took up the offer and suggested 'I personally value respect. For me respecting each other regardless of our backgrounds is a good value that we should learn both at home and at school. In fact, for me it's more important than the school curriculum, because without respect, teachers will not be able to teach us effectively to be good citizens. Respect must begin in our homes and in our schools. We must respect our parents, our friends and our teachers. If we all did that, how easy would it be for us to acquire good values? I think the good old days of school discipline should come back. Teachers need to be given more powers in dealing with students who are disruptive. Otherwise we are just stalling a big problem that might contribute to a broken society.'

'In addition to what Ndombo has just said, can I also add something please?' Marko from Spain asked *Gogo*.

'Yes, go ahead *muzukuru'*, *Gogo* encouraged him to speak out.

'I think respect is crucial and together with respect, I think communities should also have shared experiences, which is why it is important to have communal events like what you *Gogo* has been doing, by inviting all the villagers to come and help you to harvest your crops. By sharing time together, we ensure the development of mutual trust, which is foundational in creating strong communities and a healthy society. Besides, life is always better when you can share it.'

'Good point Marko, and building on what you said, why do you think communities especially in the developed world find it hard to do that?' *Gogo* quizzed him.

Laura came in next. 'Well I guess it's the fast pace of life and technology, especially the social networking sites which lead to superficial relationships. I have also realised that the media over-plays a few bad incidents and this encourages some communities to live in fear of other communities. So people would rather associate with people they know and understand while being suspicious of people who look different. They can't be bothered to learn new cultures, let alone explore areas of mutual interest. I guess someone has to take the initiative, and I guess this cultural exchange initiative arranged by you *Gogo* and Chief

102

Nehoreka will go a long way in bringing back trust into the heart of communities around the world. I hope that we can take away something from our experiences here and easily transfer the skills we have learnt back to our own communities.'

Gogo added to what Laura had said. 'Well I suppose your own society has its own strengths too. You have abundant resources, for example, community centres, public libraries, effective transport and large parks. Your challenge is to encourage people from different ethnic backgrounds to meet in those places. It might not be easy but I guess it is the little steps that make a difference. I will help you to come up with some action plans on how you can approach this issue back in your own countries. In fact, I am praying for a year when Chief Nehoreka and I can have enough resources to invite more students here to learn these *ubuntu* principles. I recently attended a workshop in Brazil where their communities use the same 'Training for life' principles, but under a different term called 'accompanier'.

The discussion continued well into the night under the African moon. In the background they could hear barking dogs from a distant, which provoked a response from *Gogo's* dogs. They could also hear the sounds of hyenas and other nocturnal animals which preyed on weaker animals. In the dark eastern side of the homestead, they also noticed a flickering flame. One of the girls asked what it was and *Gogo* said that it was probably a restless ghost looking for a resting place from the torment it was suffering in hell. It was difficult to tell whether she said

103

this in jest or not. Laura looked petrified. Then they also heard a piercing male voice singing repeatedly, *'Nyenyedzi yababa ngaigare neni* (God, may your star abide with me tonight)'. *Gogo* explained to them that the apostolic man was pleading with God for his angels to protect him during the night. The students laughed when they realised that the singing man was the same man they had likened to Rick Ross earlier in the day. While they were still laughing, a group of local men appeared from the dark wearing hunting regalia. One of them called Soropinyo began greeting *Gogo* Ndoro.

'*Eh, maswera sei Nyamuzihwa, ndimika munavo vazukuru vechingezi ava? Zvino varungu varikuhugona here upenyu uhu?* (How has been your day? Are our European visitors managing this life style?')

The men who had just been on a hunting expedition, had all sorts of wild game on their shoulders. They gave *Gogo* a well- prepared and marinated buck to roast for the young people to have as a snack before bed time.

'Have you spotted any wild pigs or monkeys on my 55 hectares of land?' *Gogo* asked the men.

One of them replied, 'No, we didn't spot any today, but we are glad that our visit to the farm was not in vain. We also got this kudu's horn. Perhaps one of your visitors might want to take it as a trophy.'

He threw the kudu's horn towards the group, which Nakai caught mid air and turned into a musical instrument called the *hwamanda*. After bidding good-bye to *Gogo* and the students, the men retreated into the dark and made their way to their respective homes. The students were very astonished by this *ubuntu* culture, which permeated every aspect of this community.

'This is a really big society,' Doug remarked.

As the young people were showing signs of weariness, Gogo sought to wind up the session by emphasizing the relationships that harmonized communities. She quipped that God gave everyone two ears and one mouth so that they would listen to others more than they would speak, and this would show that we care for others. She proceeded, 'We should choose to understand others. We should choose to intentionally connect with others in life. We should view others with a non-judgmental attitude. When we are dealing with others, let us not always think in terms of what we can benefit from the relationships, but how we can help the other persons involved. Wherever you go in life, just like Chief Nehoreka told you, you will meet people whether on your way up or on your way down. Never underestimate their potential to help you to achieve your dreams, but don't step on their shoulders to achieve your dreams. Stay positive but honest and encouraging to others. I am aware that most of you will be going to university when you go back to your respective countries. Please remain true to the principles that you have learnt here. I have no doubt that one day you will be successful in your prospective careers, but above all you will be successful as future leaders who will build a more hospitable world'. *Gogo* Ndoro then closed the session with a word of prayer, asking God to bless all the nations represented in her house that night. She also prayed for peace all over the world.

The young people pulled their tents and sleeping bags and were soon snoring under the bright African moon. As usual, when others were snoring, Doug was awake; musing on how privileged he was to be at such a place at that time.

'Now I am not surprised why Prince William regard Africa as his second home. I am sure after his wedding with Kate Middleton, he might relocate to Africa.' He looked at the three signature stars in the galaxy. In his heart, he pondered on the lyrics of the song 'Rule the world.'

> *You light, the skies up above me. A star, so bright you blind me. Don't close your eyes; don't fade away ...All the stars are coming out tonight. They're lighting up the sky tonight, for you, for you. All the stars are coming out tonight, they're lighting up the sky tonight, for you.*

***

The rest of the week went in a blur because the students had a very hectic schedule. *Gogo* had arranged cultural exchange placements with local families. They spent their time shadowing local families and community leaders, learning more about Zimbabwean culture and sharing insights from their own cultures too. *Gogo* had requested the Chinhoyi Technical College to sort out some portfolios for them where they could jot down their learning experiences and maintain a reflective journal on their progress. Some students shadowed cattle herdsmen, others shadowed a local fortune-teller called Diesel, and others shadowed a women's cooperative club. Some joined the local school basketball team, while others chose to stay with *Gogo* Ndoro. Troy chose to shadow the apostolic man. He had a lot of fun as he learnt of how western religion shaped and modified Zimbabwean cultures. The students who were placed at the Women's Club near Murombedzi were impressed to realise that the local women achieved a lot of progress with very few resources. They received funding for their irrigation projects from the government and international NGO's, which they put to very good use in growing some cabbages and other vegetables. The women exported the produce to the developed countries. There were some social workers from Harare who helped them in the planning process and taught them the principles of community development.

In the evenings the students met at *Gogo's* place as usual, and took a shower at the nearby river, and on their way back they gathered some fruits such as *nhunguru, tsvoritsvoto, chechete, tsvanzva, hute, matamba and nzviro*. Some of the students also helped *Gogo* to make cheese out of her cultured milk. The English students squeezed the juice from the fruits to make a squash they called 'Fruits of the forest'. They also shared stories and jokes, practised music together and shared ideas on best practice regarding how to build strong cohesive communities, and how to ensure that they helped other young people to value education.

Ndombo, Farai and other Zimbabwean students were especially fascinated to learn that some students in America and England who are not academically talented are allowed to concentrate on technical subjects which suit their interests, and develop skills in their areas of interest.

'These western schools are getting it right there. I don't think it is right to force students to take up Maths if they are not good at it, and in the process neglect their own God-given talents, for example, farming.' Ndombo said, with verve.

Farai agreed with her. 'I will take this issue up with the Minister of Education, Senator David Coltart in our Youth Parliament sessions. The education system that we inherited from the colonial times requires a shake up. We can't go on like this, failing students who are not academically gifted. They should be allowed to learn their chosen trades.'

When the students visited some of the local schools, the visitors were impressed by the order in the schools and how the local students valued things that most westerners would take for granted, for example, libraries. What mainly touched the visitors was that local students went to school wearing uniforms with their shirts properly tucked in. They sang the national anthem and prayed during assembly time. The teachers maintained order and were respected by students and their parents. When they left Chinhoyi, it was more than a cultural exchange tour for them. Their values and attitudes had been challenged. They were prepared to go out there and immediately implement what they had learnt. Before the left they attended the

108

unveiling of the Gogo Ndoro Public Library, which was the first of its kind in the country. Part of the library was going to accommodate the Nakai Disabled Children Arts Centre, honouring the contribution that Nakai had made to the well-being of disabled children through music from the time he recovered from mental illness. Doug made a few suggestions to ensure that the library was fully eco-friendly. He and his friends promised to donate some books as soon as they got back to their respective countries. *Gogo* had invited the Zimbabwean Minister of Education to cut the ribbon and declare the library open. The minister read his speech, the highlight of which was his explanation of the role of a public library based on the UNESCO 1994 Public Library Manifesto. In part, the minister said:

'Freedom, prosperity and the development of society and of individuals are fundamental human values. They will only be attained through the ability of well-informed citizens to exercise their democratic rights and to play an active role in society. Constructive participation and the development of democracy depend on satisfactory education as well as on free and unlimited access to knowledge, thought, culture and information.

'The public library, the local gateway to knowledge, provides a basic condition for lifelong learning, independent decision-making and cultural development of the individual and social groups.

'The public library is a living force for education, culture and information, and as an essential agent for the fostering of peace and spiritual welfare through the minds of men and women.

'UNESCO therefore encourages national and local governments to support and actively engage in the development of public libraries. The public library is the local centre of information, making all kinds of knowledge and information readily available to its users. The services of the public library should be provided on the basis of equality of access for all, regardless of age, race, sex, religion, nationality, language or social status. Specific services and materials must be provided for those users who cannot, for whatever reason, use the regular services and materials, for example linguistic minorities, people with disabilities, or people in hospitals or prisons. All age groups must find material relevant to their needs. Collections and services have to include all types of appropriate media and modern technologies as well as traditional materials. High quality and relevance to local needs and conditions are fundamental. Material must reflect current trends and the evolution of society, as well as the memory of human endeavour and imagination. Collections and services should not be subject to any form of ideological, political or religious censorship, nor commercial pressures.

'The public library's key missions which relate to information, literacy, education and culture are creating and strengthening reading habits in children from an early age; supporting both individual and self conducted education as well as formal education at all levels; providing opportunities for personal creative development; stimulating the imagination and creativity of

110

children and young people; promoting awareness of cultural heritage, appreciation of the arts, scientific achievements and innovations; providing access to cultural expressions of all performing arts; fostering inter-cultural dialogue and favouring cultural diversity; supporting oral tradition; ensuring access for citizens to all sorts of community information; providing adequate information services to local enterprises, associations and interest groups; facilitating the development of information and computer literacy skills; supporting and participating in literacy activities and programmes for all age groups, and initiating such activities if necessary.

'I would like to thank *Gogo* Ndoro for all her sterling efforts in contributing to the construction of this library. Her contributions to education, youth mentoring and lifelong learning are unparalleled. Lastly, I would like to thank our special guests today who include Laura, Kirsty and Doug to name but a few. I am sure most of you have seen them around the village during their holiday cultural exchange programme. Thank you for giving them all the support they needed. I also want to thank all the villagers who helped in any way towards the construction of the library. I sincerely hope your children will use this facility and grow up with sound values, as they are our future leaders.'

After the minister's speech, there was ululation and jubilation. The students had snacks and listened to songs such as '*Fundo inokosha kana uchiikwanisa*' a song eulogizing education.

Nakai closed the meeting with a word of prayer. In his prayer he said, 'God raise us to be children with good values, children who are grateful for your blessings. Every day, we should ask ourselves: am I expressing and receiving love? Am I open to laughter and good humour? Am I being a good friend, and am I enjoying my friends? Am I expressing and developing my talents? Am I grateful for what I have been given? Am I making a positive contribution to the world around me? Maybe with these sets of values Father, we can attain happiness and help others to do so in the process. Amen.'

Chapter 9: Matopos Hills

WHEN Sarah Rhodes carried out a casual ancestral search in her hometown library of Bishop Stortford to find out her genealogy, she was surprised to find strong evidence that she was related to Cecil John Rhodes. Visiting Zimbabwe for the training camp, therefore, gave her a further incentive to find out the extent of her ancestor's influence in Zimbabwe. Her desire to see where her ancestor had been buried was mainly motivated by the need for emotional closure. It was therefore natural that when they left Chinhoyi, she persuaded her colleagues to visit Bulawayo, Zimbabwe's second largest city. When they arrived in Bulawayo, what surprised them was that people there mostly spoke a different language from the rest of the country. Sarah sought explanation from one of the local students, Dumisani, who was part of their entourage.

'How come people here speak a very smooth language and click their tongues as they speak?' she asked.

Dumisani told her about Zimbabwe's diverse cultures and languages. He told her that the language was called Ndebele, and the other language she had heard earlier in other parts of Zimbabwe was called Shona.

'So, it's like Welsh and English then?' Sarah sought clarification.

'Sort of I should say', Dumisani responded. The number of phonemes in the Ndebele language amused Sarah and how it clicked as its people spoke. It reminded her of what she had once read that Southern Africa was the cradle of human language because languages that clicked, and that contained many phonemes, were the original humankind languages.

'By the way do you know the British singer called Jamelia?' Dumisani asked.

'Yes I know her very well,' Sarah responded.
'Well, her father comes from this city,' Dumisani added.

Sarah was further surprised by this revelation.

When they arrived in Bulawayo, they were amazed with the cleanliness of the city compared to other cities they had been to. The wide roads were well-swept. They were also impressed with the city hall especially its Victorian architecture. Later during the day, they visited the Matopo National Park where Sarah's ancestral relative was buried. They arrived on horseback under the blazing heat. The horses' hooves made noise as they came against a hard surface and some cobblestones. They rode along meandering paths that criss-crossed the national park. On either side of the paths were groves with swathes of trees that ranged from mountain acacia, wild pear trees, and the paperback. There were also many aloes, wild herbs, and over a hundred grass species. They also saw many animals ranging from the white rhinoceros, sable antelope and impala. Later, when they toured the park in a jeep, they saw many leopards. Matopo has the highest number of leopards due to the easy availability of hyrax that they feed on. As they rode on their horses, before touring in a jeep, they occasionally disembarked to give the horses water to drink along the Maleme River.

As they approached the Matopos Hills, Sarah began to weep quietly as her horse slowed down. Coming to the realization that she was right on the land where one of her ancestral relation's bones lay buried was a very emotional journey. She disembarked from her horse and followed a group of local scouts who walked slowly on old granite rocks that had since evolved to 'whaleback dwalas', and broken kopjes strewn with boulders and interspersed with thickets of vegetation. The scouts pointed towards the World View Hill Top and said in Ndebele: *'Okulele kona umlamula nkunzi ukhokho wakho uCecil John Rhodes.'*

Sarah laid a wreath, made an obeisance and prayed quietly as she made a sign of the cross. The scouts were very touched and amazed by this young girl's patriotism and respect for her heritage. They began conversing among themselves and Dumisani said, 'She is a brave girl. She wants to know where she came from. I think returning to your heritage as she is doing is very fulfilling. It is like returning to innocence'. As Dumisani spoke, the other Scouts nodded their heads in sombre agreement while at the same time respecting the significance of that moment to Sarah. Sarah collected a soil sample from where Rhodes was buried, and placed it in an urn, before putting the urn safely into her backpack. She wanted to go and donate the soil to the Cecil John Rhodes Museum in his native town of Bishop Stortford, East Hertfordshire, in England, where she lived. As she gazed at the tomb, she was transfixed into a

115

trance by the mysterious powers of the Matopos. Like someone watching a movie, her mind went back to the period when Cecil John Rhodes came to that part of the world and raised the British flag. Everything was unfolding slowly before her like a motion picture; right from the Boer Great Trek of 1835 to the time Cecil John Rhodes went to Natal to join his brother Herbert, before he crossed into Zimbabwe as part of his strong belief of the British Empire. While she was still in that trance, she began to retreat from the sight as the scouts gave her a few velvet *mupembere* leaves to wipe her teary eyes. With sudden resolve Sarah began to retreat from the place. Something made her to sing the song 'Return to innocence' by Enigma. The others joined in.

Love, devotion, feeling, emotion
Don't be afraid to be weak,
don't be too proud to be strong.
Just look into your heart my friend,
that will be the return to yourself,
the return to innocence...

She felt as if she was being featured in a time travel movie, and had been whisked back in time. She wondered what her contribution to history would have been in the 19th century. After her meditation, the scouts asked the visitors if they could also pay homage to their Ndebele ancestors who had perished during the war with Rhodes' troops. The students agreed. The scouts had been inspired by Sarah's courage and virtue in honouring her ancestral relative. They felt compelled to do the same to their ancestors as well. They leant that it was important to document and archive their history; wisdom that would perpetuate future civilizations. They realised that there is something profound, invaluable yet intangible about national history. Although there wasn't much that had been preserved in museums, libraries and ancestry websites, the Matopo Hills archived a very rich history about the early tribes who lived in the area now called Matabeleland. The San (Bushmen) had lived in the hills nearly 2000 years back, leaving a rich heritage in the form of more than 3000 rock paintings; dating back to 320 and 500 C.E. In the many crevices and caves, clay ovens and other historic artefacts had been found, and various archaeological finds dating as far back as the Pre-Middle Stone Age era; around 300,000 B.P.

Dumisani, Thandi, Themba, Siphiso as well as the other Scouts and Girl Brigades from Bulawayo scoured through the leaves and walked carefully on the dwalas until they came face to face with paintings portraying bushmen and women going about their daily errands such as hunting and preparing meals on fire in the wilderness. Dumisani and his team stood there in silence, gazing at the paintings. Dumisani and the scouts felt as if they were transported back through the passage of time, to prehistoric times. Such was the power of the Matopos magic. While in trance, the inanimate paintings gradually became animated in their imagination. The whole Ndebele group began to converse in early Ndebele dialects, Kalanga and other languages spoken in that region. It was like a motion picture. It was the same way Sarah had seen her heritage unfolding before her. The motion picture revealed a very harmonious society that observed a seamless division of labour with women carrying out the domestic work while the men went out to hunt and look for wild roots and legumes. It was a complete civilization in its own right. The picture of men hunting contradicted the findings by the University of Colorado at Boulder, which had stated that early cave men preferred to stay at home while their women ventured out. One of the American students mused over these at that moment. There were no links between this civilization with the European civilization that was eventually forced on the people when the Europeans colonized the region. They saw the civilization growing and mutating into better forms that were nowhere near the English civilization. The people looked happy and free in their own right. There appeared to be no western-type democracy but numerous small tribes, which resolved their own differences using traditional courts.

When the scouts came out of their trance they realised that what they had observed in trance was just a dream because in real life their civilization had been heavily distorted by western civilization, and life would never be the same again. Before they left the Hills, they sang the song 'God bless Africa' in Ndebele; '*Nkosi sikelela iAfrika*'. On their way down, they met Mr Nyathi, a musician and dub poet of note, and a group of European tourists. Mr Nyathi was shooting a video for the rebranding of Zimbabwean tourism called 'Zimbabwe World of Wonders'. They spoke to him and his team and proceeded on their horses to the Maleme Camp where they put up for the night. This was the main camp in the centre of the park, which hosted the park headquarters. There were self-catering facilities; eighteen lodges and six chalets, the former fully equipped and the latter with communal ablutions and without crockery or cutlery. Three of the lodges, Imbila, Black Eagle and Fish Eagle, had fantastic views over the Maleme Gorge. Imbila Lodge offered a higher standard of luxury with ensuite bathrooms and mahogany teak furniture. Camping and caravan sites were situated along the eastern shores of Maleme Dam.

The following day the students and their local hosts had a quiet 'brunch' at the Bulawayo Country Club. Breakfast comprised smoothies, then a breakfast wrap (scrambled eggs, bacon, cheddar cheese, finely chopped onion and tomato) and side salad (cucumber, lettuce and green pepper), and filtered coffee. The people around there were smiling and pleasant as usual. The students didn't speak much as they were tired since they had gone around the park looking for animals for good part of the previous day. Sarah and the local scouts and girls brigades were also ruminating on the emotional journey they had gone through the previous day. They were rewinding and trying to find a pride of place in their hearts where they could hide the pleasant yet emotional memories they had just dug from the Matopos Hills. They all felt that they had reclaimed something that had been lost for years. Somehow the things they reclaimed made them to see the necessity to redeem time and begin doing something worthwhile with their lives. They were prepared to turn the mundane into the miraculous. As they reflected in the restaurant, a radio softly played pleasant songs by the legendary Lovemore Majaivana such as *Esambeni, Mkwenyana* and *Yingwebani.* From the restaurant, the students went to view the *Umdhala Wethu* statue in the city centre before they took off for Harare, Zimbabwe's capital city.

Chapter 10: Harare

ON their way to Harare, the party decided to hire a luxury coach and travelled along the Bulawayo – Harare highway passing through the cities of Gweru and Kwekwe, and the towns of Kadoma and Chegutu. Along the way, the coach stopped in every city and town where they learnt a lot about Zimbabwe. What mainly struck the English students were the vestiges of English life and architecture in the town squares; the old town houses, town squares and government buildings. In Kadoma, Gemma Saunders who had grown up in the town of Stevenage in England made an interesting observation that Kadoma was twinned with her own town. It reminded her of a time when the Mayor of Stevenage and the Mayor of Kadoma used to pay each other annual ceremonial visits.

They came across ordinary Zimbabweans who were selling fruits, vegetables and artefacts along the roadsides. These people were very courageous and did not rely on state handouts. They were not beneficiaries of state benefits, and they had no pensions. They were making an honest living and were very cheerful under tough circumstances. The students realised how spoilt they were, coming from countries that threw away food and other necessities of life. It made them reflect on their own attitudes towards the world beyond their borders, and to re-think about their own values. However, the people they met were very generous and sensitive to them and always wished them well.

Although the highway they travelled along was not as advanced as the A roads in England, the autobahn in Germany or the Interstate Freeways in America, they had a unique advantage of flexibility and did not have unnecessary regulations. Low traffic volumes meant that community life from the villages and the cities encroached alongside the highways. Buses and cars stopped anywhere it was convenient to stop to pick up roadside travellers who needed a lift to the next town or home. Motorists did so without a second thought of being hijacked or mugged by the hitchhikers they picked up. An atmosphere of trust and a spirit of cohesion existed among complete strangers. Through talking to each other in the cars or buses, some of these strangers would find out that they were related in one way or the other, for example, if they shared a similar totem. Besides, less traffic volumes on the roads meant that the biodiversity in the bushes along the roadsides was preserved due to less polluted air in comparison with the pollution levels in the developed world.

The students arrived in Harare about midday and visited a few places such as the Lion and Cheetah Park, West Gate Shopping Centre and the suburb of Highfields. An Indian student Rajiv Patel visited a temple in Belvedere; Asif Mohamed who was Muslim visited the Ridgeview Mosque for lunch hour prayers while Doug visited a synagogue in the same location too. The Christian students also toured several churches and convents in and around Harare. Those who had an interest in the Zimbabwean African traditional religion (ART), visited *Sekuru*

Gora's homestead in Tynewald. The Chinese students were very surprised to discover a flourishing Chinese community in Harare, and the English students were equally surprised to see a huge number of white Zimbabweans of British and European origins. The students were impressed by Zimbabwe's cultural, religious and cultural diversity. Most of the young people in Harare had adopted the American culture and mixed it with their own culture, coming up with a very unique blend. In one street, you would hear a young person shouting, 'Hey what's up, are you going to Chicken Inn?' In another street you would hear a young person saying, *'Ndeipi muface, uri kupinda neipi?'* These were young people who were proud of their own culture but who also realised that the world had shrunk so much that it had become a global village and therefore they needed to adapt.

The streets of Harare were clean, and the avenues were lined with Jacaranda trees that were in full bloom. In the suburbs, the houses were very big and had extensive well-manicured gardens that were as big as UK parks. Most houses were hidden behind dense trees and bougainvillea hedges, with gardeners darting up and down moving water sprinklers around. This was invariably the case in most low-density suburbs such as Mount Pleasant, Borrowdale and Greendale. In the Avenues or the inner city, residents lived in flats and garden flats. Garden flats looked like what they would call houses in England. In the high-density suburbs such as Highfields, the houses and the yards were smaller. The houses resembled what would be detached and semi-detached houses in England, with a sizeable flower space in front and a vegetable plot at the back. The houses also had sizeable verandas mainly at the front where families and friends would meet for recreation while basking in the sun. Every neighbourhood had a dusty open space in the middle where young people played football and other sports. The sense of community was very strong. Children were playing outside until late without adult supervision. Even the dogs and chickens also wondered around without fear of local authority environmental agents.

After their tour of Harare, they proceeded to the Totem Shumba Estate in Umwinsdale where they were going to spend the night before the Christmas carol service as it was now towards Christmas. Their coach made some twists and turns along a narrow private road that passed through green thickets that harboured various animals. Kirsty asked what the place was called. She had asked the same question when they arrived from England. The coach driver slowly mouthed his words 'Umwinsidale'.

'What does that mean, if I may ask, please?' Sarah asked. The driver explained that a dale is an open river in a hilly area or it can mean a valley.

'Umwinsidale' was originally a river called 'muvhinzi' in Shona meaning a tributary but the white settlers, finding it difficult to pronounce the word, ended up changing it to 'Umwinsidale'. This was not uncommon as suburbs such as Kamfinsa in Harare originally meant a swamp with a local fruit called '*hute*'. However, some places had retained their original names such as 'Chisipiti' suburb, which means a water spring. Young Zimbabweans nevertheless pronounced these vernacular names as if they are pronouncing English names because of the influence of the English language and culture.

Their coach emerged from the road that wound through the thickets and entered a very magnificent estate with neatly- painted cottages, sparsely distributed trees and large swimming pools. On this Saturday afternoon, their hosts were sitting on a sunny patio, having a barbeque, and listening to traditional music. They had pitchers of ice-cold homemade lemonade, and several dishes of food, while a cool breeze from the Chishawasha Hills and Sugarloaf Mountain provided natural air conditioning onto the patio. They felt a sense of deep peace. There is nothing more peaceful, fulfilling and joyful than to be in sync and one with nature. Mature, healthy green-leafed Musasa trees surrounded them. The greenery of the lawn and Cuban Royals in the garden complemented the surrounds. The birds were singing their hearts out despite the soft music that wafted from the house. In that very moment, the students were alive and cherishing every second. They were like kings and queens.

The hosts welcomed their visitors with utmost hospitality and took their bags into the *cottages* (an outhouse mainly used to accommodate visitors), before they escorted them to a very large house with a huge living room that accommodated all thirty of them.

They were made comfortable and sat down to chat, drink sodas and nibble baps.

'Wow, this is like Buckingham palace!' Doug exclaimed. The students began asking a lot of questions about the exquisite artwork and ornaments that decorated the house. The affable house owner, Rumbi, was glad to answer their questions. She told them that she was actually *Gogo's* daughter. *Gogo* had organized this surprise trip to Harare for them.

'Oh! *Gogo* from Chinhoyi?' They all asked in unison.

'Yes, *Gogo* Ndoro, she is my mum. In fact, she owns her own houses here in Harare, but since she is now retired, she prefers to spend time in her rural home in Chinhoyi, organizing cultural exchange tours for students together with Chief Nehoreka. That's where her heart is. In the pursuit of her promise, she doesn't allow herself to be caught up in the trappings of destiny. She knows that life can present several opportunities and one of the greatest threats to attaining the best is when we follow what looks or feels good to our natural senses at the expense of what is best according to our hearts and souls. However, my mother did not just have that life style over night. She worked very hard over the years. In the first phase of her life, she was learning, in the second phase, she earned and now she is returning to the community. You can't return before you learn and earn because in such cases you barely have anything to return to.'

'OMG, Gogo is so special. Rumbi, which European country did you import your artwork from, please, if I may ask?'

'No, I didn't import these artworks. We manufacture these ornaments here at our estate. I will show you the workshops in a moment for you to see what I am talking about'. The young people all sat on their chairs and settees and requested Rumbi to speak at length about her wonderful works of art. Rumbi told them.

'Nothing defines a nation as much as the stylistic language of the interior of its homes. Homes are places where people live for a significant part of their lives, where characters are shaped, and a sense of style, design intelligence and respect for self is fostered. Here at Totem Shumba we believe in supporting people to make their houses into homes where their children can come of age with confidence and security. Here in Zimbabwe, we have a rich heritage of art, and it is our intention that locally made ornaments decorate every home. I am sure you noticed this with my mother who is an ardent artist in her own right. This country is blessed with a treasure trove of artistic objects to adorn homes with. Here at Totem, we also educate, inspire, inform and dispel the old general myth that antiques such as masks, clay pots, and Tonga stools are a source of evil, and that local art objects are only a preserve of rich black and white people. We want to see Zimbabwean homes telling the stories of their own god-given rich artistic heritage.

'We must cherish locally produced artistic objects that can bring glamour and glitz unique to Zimbabwe. Foreigners buy most of the home-grown handmade ornaments. Cecil John Rhodes designed his house using motifs and collections from Great Zimbabwe in Masvingo.

At the mention of Cecil John Rhodes, Sarah almost jumped to her feet but had to calm herself. Rumbi noticed it but simply thought Sarah was feeling uncomfortable as she had been sitting for a long time, so she continued with her speech.

'When I set up this collectibles gallery, I was inspired by an ancient spirit in my soul, and I am determined to change the current belief system by showcasing artistic items that can be used to beautify homes and offices. I am an avid collector of Zimbabwean antiques, as I believe that there's so much beauty in locally produced artwork; beauty that can bring local home interiors to life with grace and style. There is a great need for self-definition and self-knowledge that is currently catching up between both the old and young generations alike. Our items, mostly made from wrought iron, range from candleholders to metal chairs, and have a graphic quality to them that is stunning yet functional. The large variety of accessories we have can add a finishing touch which is uniquely Zimbabwean, to homes, and tell a story of the beauty of our local artists' minds. A lack of appreciation for our own art is partly a legacy of colonialism, and a form of religion that fosters a collective psyche of self-loathe for things indigenous.

'We are collaborating with young, upcoming artists and the less privileged families to produce the art works. As Africans, we're stuck in the middle. We're westernised yet we are not western enough, and at the same time we're

African but not completely African. We are a social hybrid. I think it's a lack of self-knowledge that makes people hate their own art works. The belief that local objects were tinted with evil constituted the main deterrent for Zimbabweans to creatively design the interiors of their homes using locally available resources. While we Zimbabweans are able to move from one world to another, the problem is that we easily become compartmentalized. We tend to be copycats. We are too comfortable in our self-defined boxes that we do not take to creative interior design. Take leather sofas, for example, most people want leather sofas in their homes just because it's regarded as a status symbol despite the fact that they're quite uncomfortable. It's important to realize that steadiness and permanence is found in willingness to experiment and change. When I look at locally produced collectibles, I immediately see visions of the past; I see the richness of my history. With the Tonga stools in my collection, I can almost hear the Tonga people of the past singing. It makes me appreciate my heritage, helping me to know who I am.'

When Rumbi mentioned this, the Ndebele scouts saw the resemblance with their experiences at the Matopos, where they observed inanimate rock paintings come to life.

On the other hand, Troy thought of the Tonga people he had met in Matusadonha. Rumbi continued. 'It is important for interior decoration to reflect one's identity, and should be designed using collectibles that can be passed from one generation to the next as part of heritage. Decorating and design is fuelled by a sense of renewal and a quest for change. Our homes should reflect the depth of our traditional values and culture. Tell me, what do we have in our homes to pass on to the next generation? In other parts of the world, they collect these pieces and pass them on to the next generation. As for me, I love spaces and I can work with form and shape. When a space is not talking to me, it must change. I will modify a space until it begins talking to me.

I bring together different artists – my idea is to promote young people. We try to provide world-class quality products at a low cost. We don't believe in the culture of ripping off others, which has infected this country. In the process, we are creating new jobs and contributing to the future. The future of Zimbabwe is our own hands.

'It's high time we become proud of our artistic heritage and culture. Foreigners buy most of our products yet we could be using them to enrich our own souls. We need to create awareness that we can beautify our homes using locally produced artworks. This estate is testament to my lifelong desire to celebrate my creative spirit and natural self. I've always yearned to do something creative. My father did not support venturing into the arts because he was not sure how arts could help to bring food on the table. After I spent some years outside the country, when I came back I knew I wanted to do something in the creative realm. I'm so much in touch with nature, I like all things natural. It is an acceptance of who I am.'

The students gave Rumbi a round of applause for her speech, which accorded very well with what they had already learnt elsewhere especially in Masvingo and Chinhoyi.

After this passionate presentation, the students were free to wander around the estate. Doug did quite a lot of painting of the landscape, but other students chose to swim. A few others took a drive around Mazowe Citrus Estate and came back in time for dinner. Before bedtime, the Romantic Trio regrouped to prepare for the following day's Christmas performances that were going to take place at the City Cathedral. They were joined by local children for the rehearsals. Doug spotted a piano that was dumped in one of the rooms and asked for Rumbi's permission to play it. He played it while the rest of the students and his hosts gazed in amazement. The scene he created was reminiscent of the day when Brahms visited the Schumanns in 1853. As Doug played, his well-chiselled features shone under the light provided by the setting sun. His imposing figure underwent a transfiguration as he filled the whole house with music, thus mirroring the portrait of Jesus' Transfiguration, hanging on the opposite wall from where he was sitting. Doug demonstrated a depth of feeling and imagination which suggested that he had only been born to play the piano. The artistic and serene environment at Rumbi's Estate provided him with inspiration to a point that he wanted to continue playing until the moon set. When Nakai, who had been walking among the Msasa trees, heard Doug's piano, he brought out the kudu horn he had brought from Chinhoyi, and blew it as he joined in. When Doug was climaxing, Nakai stopped to allow the piano sound to go uninterrupted. When Doug finished playing, his guests who had been overwhelmed by his genius gave him a glass of orange juice and allowed him time to rewind as he sat on the bench outside watching the moon's reflection in the swimming pool in front of him. Whilst in deep meditation, he heard the sound of an African drum, and the sound increased in intensity as the breeze from the Chishawasha Hills became stronger. As he subsequently learnt, the drumbeat was coming from St Dominic's Girls' School behind the mountains. The nuns there were rehearsing in readiness for the Christmas Catholic mass. Doug felt the energy from both the drumbeat and from the moon energising him, clearing his mind and giving him a new perspective that there was a happy world out there beyond his narrow confines of Twickenham. He came back from his daydreaming when a ripe apple dropped from the overhanging branch with a thud right in front of him. He felt at peace within, and did not feel the urge to run away, or to be edgy, as he had always felt before the tour. Rumbi's gardens were like the Garden of Eden.

* * *

When they arrived at the Harare City Cathedral, the church hall was already packed. The rest of the students went into the main gallery to mingle with other students and their families. The Romantic Trio went backstage together with a couple of other students who were also going

132

to be performing. After a number of nativity performances by local children and their parents, the Romantic Trio performed Tchaikovsky's Nutcracker- the magical story of the young girl Clara's Christmas Eve dream in which her nutcracker doll becomes a Prince, and whisks her away to the Kingdom of sweets. The Trio had to simplify it since they didn't have all their instruments and an adequate number of choreographers. However they harmonised sound, dance, and music to come up with a spectacular play. They displayed a very specialised and subtle technique, which pleased aspiring local ballerinas.

This was followed by many songs, which they all sang together. Some of the songs included 'Pausiku hweutsvene (Silent Night). They sang the local version, and the version by Frank Sinatra. They also sang Cliff Richard's Millennium Prayer', Mary's Son, The Idol's 'This is Christmas, and many other great Christmas carols. Finally, four students who had come from Vienna teamed up with a local student from Kutama College who was a veteran chimukubhe (local flute) player, to play Schubert's fifth symphony. The symphony's youthful spontaneity and enchanting melodies befitted the moment and the youthful audience. In the same way Shubert could have done it, they played it light and in its original pastoral tempo. When the small orchestra opened the first movement with charm and spontaneity, the hall was filled with so much love and gaiety. They felt bound together by multicultural chords of love that couldn't be broken. The orchestra with its oboes, bassoons, horns and strings,

133

struck a seamless harmony with the local flute. It could have reminded one of the Vienna street songs and yet could also have reminded one of a shepherd boy playing his flute in the Murombedzi plains of Zimbabwe. They graciously and forcefully built the music through the second theme to the exposition section until it softly reached the development stage with remote keys for the recapitulation. When it ended, there were conversations in lower voices, in the hall, from the audience as they left the Cathedral, making their way into the open courts under the white and bright African moon.

The following day, the students were all over the place buying souvenirs. They attended a Christmas Bazaar in the Harare Gardens near the Meikles Hotel and also had a chance to visit a makeshift Santa's Grotto at the East Gate Shopping Complex. They visited Chinyaradzo Children's Home and donated some Christmas cuddlies, shoebox gifts and cash. The children there were very thrilled, and had some photos taken together with the students. They also had an opportunity to tour the John Bredenkemp Computer Centre at Prince Edward School where they also had a chance to watch a rugby game between the Tigers and Churchill bulldogs.

Chapter 11: Zimbabwe Eastern Highlands

THE following day they left Harare by road, back to Chimanimani, where they would pass through the Halfway House, Trout Beck Inn, St Augustine's Mission School, the city of Mutare and the Leopard Rock Motel in Vumba before heading back to Chimanimani to bid farewell to their hosts.

After a fun-filled journey from Harare with several stops in Marondera, Macheke, Headlands and the Half Way House, they arrived at the Trout Beck Inn in Nyanga where they spent a night. Along the road to Nyanga, they saw sprawling villages with thatched huts, fields, roaming animals and people, just as they had seen on their way from Bulawayo. They occasionally came across shopping centres, most which comprised one or two grocery shops, a grinding mill, and a pub (bottle store). In some instances they saw one or more men dancing to local music at the shops, while a few people watched as they sat there sipping their lagers. Almost every grocery shop had a big Coca Cola sign on its front, showing the international influence that the coca-cola brand enjoyed. In Marondera they had a stop over to see the famous nameless tree (*Mutiusinazita*). Along the way they also overtook very big haulage trucks. When Doug asked one of the locals what those trucks were carrying, he was told that some carried agricultural produce while others carried black granite rock from Mutoko, the very same rock used to make kitchen tops in western countries. A few of the trucks were carrying uncut diamonds. Doug was amazed at how wealthy Zimbabwe was in terms of its natural resources.

'Surely this is where my mother's expensive granite kitchen top was mined!' He exclaimed. When they arrived in Nyanga they were engulfed by an overwhelming serenity and captivated by the topography and the beauty of the area. The Inn was situated right among a grove of magnificent pine trees in the vicinity of trout-filled mountain streams. Close to the Inn were several amenities that included a restaurant, golf course, tennis and squash courts, and facilities for clay pigeon shooting, swimming, horse riding and fishing. Their rooms overlooked the golf course and a private lake, and all rooms were entirely self-contained and stylishly furnished.

Since they were going to have an unstructured afternoon and evening before proceeding on their journey, they were all over the place picking and choosing what they liked to do best. As the sun was about to set, some of the students including the Romantic Trio went to the World View on the Nyanga Mountain, Zimbabwe's highest mountain. They found the scenery very striking in its variety, with deep valleys, gorges, bare granite peaks, pine-forested slopes and streams bubbling with trout fish rolling down steep cliffs. They could see as far as their eyes could allow them right up to the horizon. On one side they could see the City of Mutare's Christmas Pass, and on the other side they could see Zimbabwe's border with

Mozambique, as well as criss-crossing streams, villages, animals and several fascinating features of the land. They couldn't contain their excitement so they began to sing and shout just to gauge how far their voices could go.

They felt a sense of power high up the mountain, a feeling that they could conquer the world. The local students ran around singing *'Dai ndiine mapapiro ndaibhururuka'* meaning 'If I had wings I could fly away'. On the other hand the American students sang 'I believe I can fly, I believe I can touch the sky, take my wings and fly away' while the English students shouted, 'Beautiful people where are you?', and their voices echoed in the valleys and gorges underneath. When the young local boys and girls who were busy fishing trout near the Ngororombe gorge heard this, they tried to figure out where the voices where coming from. 'Beautiful people where are you? They thought carefully before they responded, 'We are here'. They made their way to the Mountain View where the voices where coming from. They introduced themselves to the students and told them, 'Here we are, and we are the beautiful people you were calling'. The students were amused that the lyrics of their songs had been taken literally in that way. However they were glad to meet local children. They all began shouting out of excitement in different languages of the world; represented by different cultures present on the mountain. However, as the voices rose into the Honde and Nyanga valleys, only one compelling voice could be heard. This was a united voice of love from the children of all nations. Love united them because the voice of love knows neither boundaries nor colour, but speaks of only one thing- that we are beautifully and wonderfully made in God's own image.

Meanwhile, as Kirsty was watching the amazing scenery, she began to connect with nature on a deeper level. She longed to be part of this amazing landscape and wished she could just escape some of the sorrows and pressures associated with the urban life style that she had lived all her life. She felt so far away from home, yet she felt so close to herself. That was how therapeutic this environment was to her. She became very hopeful and felt all her fears vanishing. She embraced her friend Laura and they both began to sob. They were not sobbing out of sorrow or anxiety, but theirs were tears of joy which drained the residues of pain and sorrow from within. As hot tears welled in their eyes, they felt the healing power of nature. From the vantage point where they were standing, they saw very distant lands. They realised that there was a world out there filled with hope, and a life worth living and celebrating despite life's shortcomings.

As they mediated, they each felt that instead of focussing on their pains and what is perceived to be disabilities, they needed to focus on the hope the world offers. They felt that they needed to see the big picture and regain a sense of perspective. Healing and greatness lay within them, but there are some environments that have the ability to draw out that greatness and healing. During moments of solitude and loneliness people can truly appreciate the power of nature to nurture them. They felt that although the company of others is very essential and their instruction even more vital, sometimes people underestimate the power of solitude and the greatness of nature as an instructor.

The human body was born with the power to renew, replenish and heal itself but the environment has to be right. It has to reinforce that sense of hope and foster a new perspective that life offers more than meets the eye. Life should be a quest for self-discovery and also a discovery of those things that are not obvious to the eye that, if properly used, can make this world a better place.

The other students left them as the two reflected on self-discovery. When it was getting darker, Kirsty felt as if she heard a voice from a distance saying, 'I was there the whole time, I was there on the horizon, I was there but you didn't seek me out, I was within you but you did not reach right inside yourself to see me and to try me out. From today you will never blush with shame, you will reach out to the sky, and as you walk, you will look at the horizon'. She wondered whether this was a real voice or just a hallucination, but whatever it was, it must have been her moment of serendipity as she felt impeccable peace beyond comprehension, right there on the Nyanga Mountain. This was a form of peace that had evaded her in her hometown and even in the charming hills of Shropshire. This was surely Kirsty and Laura's moment. As she was still puzzled by the voice that she heard, a white mist began to build on the mountain peak where she was. She figured a silhouette of a man in the mist. The voice from the silhouette assured her that everything was going to be all right. She didn't see the man's face but the impeccable peace she felt gave her an assurance that she had had an encounter with providence in the same way Nakai had had his moment a few years earlier in the Chimanimani wilderness. Kirsty's experience could not be explained as a consequence of childhood or adolescence trauma. It could not be explained by the psychological narrative that all artists go through such experiences; which are known as possession by the sacred when they suddenly feel that their whole life is justified, their sins forgiven and that love is still the strongest force that can transform them forever. It was more than that. It was a divine encounter but the conditions had to be right. Just like Elijah, the old Hebrew Prophet, she only heard that small and still voice because the conditions were right. As Kirsty and Laura slowly began to descend from the mountain, Kirsty began to sing 'How Great though Art' and was joined by Laura:

When through the woods and forest glades I wander and hear the birds sing sweetly in the trees;
when I look down from lofty mountain grandeur, and hear the brook, and feel he gentle breeze;
Then sings my soul, my Saviour God, to Thee, How great Thou art, how great Thou art!
Then sings my soul, my Saviour God, to Thee, How great Thou art, how great Thou art!

As they passed by some quiet water ponds, Kirsty gazed into the clear water while crouching at one of the ponds to wash her face. As she did that her bright eyes shone back to her and she felt an unaccustomed surge of pride and a great sense of relief. Her skin was flawless and tanned and contrasted with the rich chestnut hair, which swept back from her fine boned oval face. A spark of intelligence in her almond-shaped eyes shifted her looks from mere prettiness to an arresting wild beauty.

***

Meanwhile the local boys and girls who had emerged from the forest were at the river showing the students how to fish the Zimbabwean way. They caught many fish but the visiting students threw theirs back into the river, because they were just fishing for fun and recreation. When it became dark, the locals bade farewell to the students and took their catch back home where their parents were anxiously waiting for the fish to supplement their evening meal. When the rest of the students were fishing, Sarah Rhodes took a walk in the Rhodes National Park. She also took the opportunity to visit the Rhodes Hotel and Museum where her ancestral relative once lived.

The Rhodes National Park is one of the oldest parks in Zimbabwe, established as Rhodes Inyanga National Park, a bequest from Cecil Rhodes. The original park's borders used to extend beyond the Udu Dam, along the east bank of the Nyangombe River to the north of the new boundary. While in solitude, Sarah had time to reflect upon and gather more evidence on her relative's lifestyle and influence in Rhodesia. She found answers to several questions that were bothering her when she left the Matopos National Park. She rummaged through some artwork and implements that had been preserved since 1902 in the Museum. She looked closely at Cecil's portraits that graced the museum. While gazing at the main portrait, like one in trance, she felt as if the portrait was smiling at her and urging her to be courageous. In that moment of solitary reflection, it was as if the portrait was saying, 'We came, we saw and we conquered'. Rhodes's finely- chiselled face and pointed nose also bore strong resemblance with her features so much that she felt she couldn't have been mistaken that they were related by blood. The lessons she learnt during that moment of solitude in the museum's gallery equipped her with history about her cultural heritage, her ancestors' successes and failures. She could not have learnt all that from anyone, even from the most experienced Historian on Rhodesia such as Jim Latham and others. She began to appreciate the significance of museums and galleries. She learnt that although some of the statues portrayed people who were dead and gone, these people's emotions and legacy remained behind and were indelible. People may try to falsify history or fight history, but for as long as people have museums and galleries, the truth can always come to light. Sarah, therefore, felt that she was equipped to face life with courage and bravery in the same way her ancestors had come to Zimbabwe to erect foundations of western civilization when the country was still a mere cluster of scattered kingdoms. As she turned her head away from the portrait and headed towards the exit door, she came face to face with Robert Mugabe's portrait. She smiled at it with the typical English *plastic* smile, and Robert Mugabe appeared to wink back.

***

The following day, they were all adorned in white and walked the stretch between the Christmas Pass and the Leopard Rock, near Zimbabwe's border with Mozambique. They were now in thousands together with other Zimbabwean kids, clutching roses and united in one message of love and upholding the values they all cherished. They were singing songs of love and peace such as *'Ranaka zuva iro;* Michael Jackson's 'Heal the world'; and 'Send it on' by Miley Cyrus, Selena Gomez, Demi Lovato and Jonas Brothers; and 'When will I see you again by The Three Degrees. As they sang 'Send it on' they mouthed the following words reflectively and conscientiously:

Send It On

A word's just a word 'Til you mean what you say And love isn't love. 'Tilyou give it away We've all gotta give Yes, something to give, To make a change Send it on, on and on. Just one hand can heal another
Be a part, reach a heart Just one spark starts a fire With one little action
The chain reaction will never stop
Make it strong. Shine a light, and send it on...

Just smile and the world will smile along with you. That small act of love

143

Is meant for one who will become two
If we take the chances, To change
circumstances, Imagine all we can do.

They had been joined by the African children's Choir from Chipinge and several students from around the country. When they were touring other parts of the country, Chief Nehoreka and Gogo Ndoro and a few Mutare City Councillors had been hectic coordinating and organising the students' Grand Finale in the Eastern Highlands. The celebrations began from Mutare Christmas Pass, a mountain pass that leads into the city of Mutare in Zimbabwe. The pass was so named by some of the colonial pioneers who camped at the foot of the pass on Christmas Day 1890. The view of the city, from the pass, is spectacular. The students joined hands and formed a very long and meandering procession, stretching from the city of Mutare through to the Vumba Mountains. The Zimbabwean procession joined the Mozambican procession, which went as far as the town of Manica in Mozambique, past the Chikangwe Dam. They all sang the song 'Send it on', quietly, and reflectively, as they were making a commitment to help make this world a better place in which all children would grow of age securely and confidently. They had placards which encouraged volunteering, the abolition of child labour, recruiting child-soldiers, the end to poverty, and others topical issues.

Chief Nehoreka, *Gogo* Ndoro, *Gogo* Boriwondo, and other old wise men and women whom they had mobilised from all over the country, and from Mozambique, were seen going this way and that way, liaising with the local police to ensure that there was minimal disruption to traffic along the highways. The organizers demonstrated that old age is not a hindrance.. Their grey hair symbolised wisdom, and they all wore neon coloured jackets. The students' perception of age, based on ageism, was challenged as they saw many elderly people contributing meaningfully to noble causes. The Council of Elders, as they were known, were also giving out bottled water distilled from the Eastern Highlands Springs, to students since the weather was very hot.

In the afternoon they all walked slowly towards the Vumba Mountains for the final Leopard Rock Concert. They came across women who were fetching firewood singing a local version of the Mamma mia song. When the women saw this sea of students all dressed in white, they were amazed and thought they had seen angels. They almost ran away until Chief Nehoreka blew a whistle and stopped them, assuring them that this was an innocent international gathering of students who were on their way to the Camp Rock Concert and Musical at the Leopard Rock. After this assurance, the women put their firewood down, still singing songs of praise, and joined the procession of students. All the people who were on their respective errands either collecting water, mushrooms or herding cattle and goats left what they were doing to join the students' procession of peace and solidarity. It was like a herd or groupie instinct as this wave of love swept across the Eastern Highlands.

Within an hour, they had all arrived at the foot of the Vumba Mountains. Those who were too weak to walk had been ferried by the local Tenda buses, or on local herdsmen's sledges and scotch-carts. As the students arrived at the Vumba Mountains, they were amazed by the magnificence of the mountains. The place was very serene. The weather was ideal. A warm sun's rays penetrated through the thickets and tree canopies. The greenery was very amazing, and it was as if the place hadn't been visited by a lot of people that summer. Even the locals, who had always taken this mountain range for granted, saw it in a new light on that day.

The mountains provide a natural border between Zimbabwe and Mozambique, and are approximately 25 kilometres south east of the City of Mutare. These mountains rise to Castle Beacon at 1911 metres. Together with the Chimanimani and Nyanga, where the students had already visited, form part of the Eastern Highlands in Zimbabwe, on the border with Mozambique. The mountains are known as the mountains of mist, because Bvumba comes from the Shona word 'Mubvumbi'. The early mornings start with mist, which clears by mid morning. These cool green hills shelter country hotels, a casino and golf course at the Leopard Rock Hotel and Botanical Gardens with one of the best views in Africa. The mountains are also known for their coffee plantations. The climb to the prominence, Castle Beacon, is up a large granite dome. The lower slopes are a mist belt with sub-montane vegetation. Proteas are found on the higher levels. Vumba Mountain, on the Mozambique side, is a steep hike to a summit

146

with a good view of Manica and environs. The Vumba Mountains are composed mainly of granite, being the eastern margin of the Zimbabwe craton. The Vumba granite has been dated at over 2600 Ma. Umkondo dolerite sills, of around 1110 Ma, intrude the granites in places.

The mountains are dominated by savannah woodland, including *Brachystegia* and *mitondo*. There are also extensive sub-montane grasslands, local mist-belts with mosses and epiphytic and lithophytic ferns, and sub-montane evergreen forest in the deeper ravines. The higher levels of the mountains are sparsely vegetated, with shrubs such as proteas, aloes and Strelitzia. In the centre of the mountains lies the Bunga Forest Botanical Reserve and neighbouring Bvumba Botanical Garden. The latter is landscaped around a number of small streams and includes an important cycad collection, with 59 of the 189 known species, including *Encephalartos manikensis*. Although small in area, the mountains are a botanical paradise and home to some of the rarest butterflies in the region. The Vumba Mountains offer exciting and varied birding opportunities. The area is probably best known as one of the main breeding areas of Swynnerton's robin, which lives and breeds in small patches of forest, some on private land, others within the Bunga forest. A smaller number of mammals inhabit the Bvumba, perhaps the most notable of which are the leopard and the *samango* monkey; the latter's range being very limited. Savannah woodland adjoining the Mozambique side of the range is home to several rare reptiles·

When the students were busy scouring the mountain taking some pictures and collecting rare stones with the help of the locals, Chief Nehoreka's technical team was busy setting up musical instruments for the concert at the Leopard Rock- a very big rock near the Leopard Rock Hotel. They were preparing the best of all gigs to mark the end of the students' tour of Zimbabwe. They had brought together some local Zimbabwean artists, including The Churchill Boys Pied Pipers, The Chitakatira Leopards, Roosevelt Pangolins, Guinea Fowls, and The Ammunition girls from Harare, Oliver Mtukudzi, the African Children Choir, Boys Dzesimoko, The Tisu Anhu Acho Band, Wasu Band and many other acts. The American students were going to perform a few bits from their High School musical. Students from Austria would perform some of Mozart's symphonies together with English students who would also perform songs by Cold Play, Spice Girls and Girls Aloud. Three Russian girls were going to re-enact the Tatu girls' 'The things she said'. Chipawo was going to perform '*Mutambo wepanyika*' play in which God is a theatre director and the World is his stage manager. The play was a reflection about life, religion and death.

As hoards of students arrived at the scene, Chief Nehoreka and his Council felt they needed students to help in coordinating the events to ensure that the camp ran smoothly. He called for silence and informed the students that he required student leaders who could help his team. He asked them how they wanted the leaders to be chosen. All the students agreed to

148

choose leaders through a ballot box. Those who were interested were asked to write their names on small pieces of paper, which were then put in a hat. Students were going to secretly vote for the leaders, but at that point boys from rival schools began to plot against each other to ensure that they would get more votes from the girls. When *Gogo* Ndoro realised the plot, she told the students to relax since not everything in life should be a competition. When two boys form Guinea Fowl, three girls from Chitakatira and three students from St Ignatius were chosen, there was tension, but the students eventually realised that tolerance was a necessary virtue in team building, and they swallowed their pride and followed orders from the chosen students. They knew that one day their chance to lead would also come, maybe not at the camp, but back at their own respective schools. *Gogo* told them that 'Some days we win but some days we lose and its okay, that's what democracy is about.'

Soon after the elections a busload with students from a special school arrived at the camp. The students had one or multiple disabilities, and found it very difficult to socialise with others. When one of the able bodied students noticed them arriving, he thoughtlessly suggested that they should be turned away as they wouldn't be able to cope with the camp's physical activities. When the chief overhead this, he was shocked by such an attitude from this student leader.

'*Chingamidza hama yako kana iyine nhamo, rega kuponda,*' The chief reproached the student. Unbeknown to the guy who had made the negative remark about disability, and to others who were at the camp, some of the students on the cultural exchange programme had different disabilities, but lived fulfilling lives because society accepted and appreciated them.

'All you need to do is to make reasonable adjustments to accommodate them,' Kirsty suggested. The student leader eventually apologised. Chief Nehoreka and the leader invited village expert builders to redesign and construct some ramps, wide entrances for wheel chairs and ensure that the place was safe enough for the disabled students. They quickly erected makeshift disabled toilets and put some disabled signs all over to ensure that the disabled students would feel welcome. Doug did the architectural designs and led the team in implementing the plan. Chief Nehoreka was amazed and suggested that he would invite Doug again to Zimbabwe to recommend his ideas to the government's department of social welfare.

As the preparations for the final Leopard Rock Musical concert were taking place, the students were scattered all over the green turf, on the Leopard Rock, and in the forest. Some were pitching tents; some were swimming while others simply chose to hang out having snacks, chatting, kicking back and relaxing. Chief Nehoreka climbed the Leopard Rock and surveyed the area with a pair of binoculars to ensure that the students were safe. From a distance, he observed a troop of students who were coming from the Mozambican side of the border. He also observed scattered leopards that were enjoying a meal in the heart of the forest.

After this, he threw a few grains of sand into the air and appeared to be measuring something. When the visiting students asked the locals what the chief was doing, they were told that he was measuring the wind speed, the air moisture and humidity levels to establish whether it would rain and the direction of the wind so that all those factors could be taken into account when setting up the tents. 'Wow, that's a wise chief,' one of the students exclaimed in amazement.

***

The naturally inspiring environment made the students feel they were on top of the world. As they sat there, the clouds glided effortlessly and silently, and occasionally they would sight blue duikers darting across the front lawn into the growth! Kirsty retreated to the other side of the Leopard Rock Hotel and sat in the serene garden. She realised that here were no distractions, no sounds of chaotic city life drifting in. This garden is vast, and nothing intrudes on its peace. Better yet, your mind is clear of worries, your body untroubled by any trace of illness, allergies, or pain. Your sense is free to take in your surroundings. You feast your eyes first on the vivid hues of the blossoms, the sparkle of a stream, the myriad greens of foliage and grass in sun and shadow. You feel the mild breeze on your skin and smell the sweet fragrances it carries. You hear the rustling leaves, the splash of water tumbling over rocks, the calls and songs of birds, the hum of insects at work.

Nakai came to where Kirsty was as the soft piano sound of the song, 'I will never see you again' slowly wafted from the hotel lobby. Nakai began to talk to Kirsty about their experiences on the tour.

'Sorry to interrupt your quiet time,' he said.

'It's okay. I have just been trying to reflect on the whole experience. It's been absolutely amazing but good things have to come to an end so they say.'

'Sure they do but I guess we are going back home with loads of life lessons, and I have no doubt these can be invaluable as we take the next steps in our career lives. I hadn't managed to learn much about you,' Nakai said suggestively.

'Well, there isn't much to know about me really. I am just a simple girl from London. I have my own struggles, hopes and aspirations.'

'What do you mean you have your own struggles? You look like pretty, fine, and privileged girl to me,' Nakai said teasingly.

'Well, you can say that, but can you believe it that when I came for this tour I had struggled with depression for a very long time, and that I feel very well now. I just can't believe it. I hope it stays that way.'

'I am truly amazed because it didn't show at all,' Nakai responded. 'You behaved and looked fine, and besides, you are such talented girls. So what do you think happened to you then?'

'Well, I am not sure really, but I guess it was a combination of factors really, from a change in environment, interacting with people who do not make you aware of your condition, organic food, the warm environment and well, although I don't

152

believe in miracles, I somehow think it was a miracle. You remember that day at Nyanga when you left Laura and me on top of the mountain?'

'Yes I do,' said Nakai. 'So tell me, what happened in Nyanga?'

'Well, I am not very sure, but a certain man whose face I couldn't exactly figure out appeared to me from a mist and assured me that I was going to be fine. It was sort of like surreal, magical and suddenly I saw my life right in front of me being dissected into piecemeal. I felt this amazing peace. Somehow I did not speak with this guy and when the mist retreated, he sort of like left. From that day I kind of feel as if I reclaimed a lost part of me. It's as if I am born again and have been given a second chance to live my dreams. I had been very hard on myself. My life was performance driven, trying to compensate for my disability but now I have forgiven my past and I am ready to embrace the future with all the promises it holds.'

As Nakai listened to this amazing encounter, his memory raced several years back when he had a similar encounter in the Chimanimani wilderness, but he didn't want to interrupt Kirsty. Kirsty continued. 'My perception on life has completely changed. I feel happy and more alert and am sure life has some amazing stuff for me.'

'What sort of things do you think life has in store for you Kirsty?'

'Well, hopefully when I go back I will start a Mental Disability Charity which equips young people living with mental illness. I want them to have control over their lives and seek alternative forms of healing. I believe God created perfect beings and when the body goes wrong, I now believe there is a way it can correct itself but this all depends on our core beliefs and attitudes. If we grow up being told that there is something wrong with us we end up believing it too even if it's a lie.'

'So do you believe in God then?' Nakai asked.

'Yes I do although I am still sceptical about miracles.'

'But it appears you just had one,' Nakai suggested.

'Well, if you say so, then I believe,' Kirsty responded, and continued. 'I also intend to pursue music as a profession and hopefully play in Austria, New York Broadway and other notable places in my home city of London. When I graduate, I would like to travel again before I start a family. I want to see the world and to enjoy my youth. There is no pressure to having a family early. Babies can wait because at this stage in my life my focus is on books and not boobs!'

'What sort of person would you like to settle with?' Nakai asked. Before Kirsty replied, she pointed out to a fern plant that was growing on a tree trunk.

'Can you see that? Can you see that a fern is growing in the most unlikely place? It's more like the flame lilies we saw, was it in Chinhoyi, which flourished and bloomed on dry ground.'

'What are you implying?' Nakai asked inquisitively.

'Well, like a fern on the trunk of that tree, love grows in most unlikely places. Like black sheep among white sheep, God puts the lonely in families. So you never know who that person might be although I would prefer someone who understands the struggles I have gone through. Skin colour doesn't matter, but I want a man who completes my strength, who makes enormous demands on me, who does not doubt my courage or my toughness, who does not believe me naive or innocent, who has the courage to treat me like a woman. Like one writer once said *'Being deeply loved by someone gives you strength, while loving someone deeply gives you courage.'*

'Wow, that's profound,' Nakai said in amazement.

'Well I guess we have to be going now, I am sure others are waiting for us and the Chief might be wondering where we have gone.'

They hugged and Nakai kissed the air on both sides of Kirsty's cheeks. They walked quietly back to where the other students were, as the piano sound seemed to fade with every meter they walked. This brief conversation had given them both a window of opportunity to see into each other's heart. Kirsty was an open and courageous girl, and Nakai was a strong boy who listened. Both of them had had serendipitous encounters. Had a seed of love been planted in their lives? Only fate would tell. Whatever would subsequently happen, Nakai smiled continuously that day when he thought of the words, 'Love grows in the most unlikely places,. Instead of hearing the music from the piano, all he heard was the deep music from the soul of Kirsty. On the other hand, Kirsty kept on hearing music from Nakai's soul. That's how people fall in love- if they hit a similar cord and if the music hidden deep down in their souls is either from the same sheet of hymn or if they can understand each other's inner song, the language of the song doesn't matter. It was more like what they call sympathetic resonance in music. If you have two pianos in the same room and you hit a B note on one piano, you will find that the B string on the other piano will start vibrating at the same rate.

***

After the gig, Doug retreated into his hotel room and took time to reflect as he went through his reflective journal and learning portfolio that *Gogo* Ndoro had bound together for him. As he thoughtfully reflected, he felt that the whole trip particularly the Leopard Rock, had been a worthwhile. From his room he could see different animals ranging from *nyala, kudu,* zebra, wildebeest as well as eland and impala. As he sat there on the window seal, he reflected on the whole event and realised that in life, times of serenity far removed from our daily suffocating and meaningless routines is essential for the replenishing of the soul. When all the superfluous things in life have been discarded, we discover simplicity and concentration. The simpler and more sober the posture, the more beautiful it will be, even though, at first, it may seem uncomfortable. When we step out of our normal world and leave behind prejudices and all the usual barriers we tend to be more adventurous within and without. We push back limiting cultural boundaries. He was amazed that although he had come to Africa with an attitude that he would teach the locals some moral values, he ended up being taught about the world around and inside him. He found healing in the process. He found himself and became a better person. He realised that each of us contains something within us which is unknown, but which, when it comes to the surface, is capable of producing miracles because greatness lies within although that greatness can be culturally construed as madness. He also felt that the secret to a happy life is found in changing the way we look at the ordinary because life is a series of ordinary events that become a collective mystery. Some of our days in this world are exciting but some days are ordinary. The secret is to make sure that our happiness is not determined by external circumstances. We can transform even the most dull days and tasks by taking them as opportunities to have an encounter with ourselves or with something higher than us which is why the Jewish King David once said, 'When my heart is overwhelmed, please take me to a rock that is higher than I.' In the same way David said these words, probably in the Judean wilderness; Doug's experiences in the forests of Zimbabwe had indeed lifted him up to a rock that was higher than him. From that vantage point, he not only managed to see the big Zimbabwean society but he saw right within himself. From that vantage point he discovered his heritage, identity, purpose, potential and destiny.

From that vantage point, he realised that deep inside every person's soul is a place of virtue, a palace, a completely unspoilt sanctuary; the size of the space differs from person to person. When the soul begins its life, this untouched space is filled with light and divine promise. The space is pure and the promises real. When we allow people to enter, to occupy, to invade and conquer our sanctuary, something is lost. We could lose our integrity, self worth, talent, promises and more. We begin to live our lives to fulfil the expectations and opinions of the squatters inhabiting our souls. When Doug had allowed people to enter his soul and judge him to be mentally unstable, he lost something, but he had recovered that 'something' during the Zimbabwean expedition

He reflected on his encounter with Chief Nehoreka and how the encounter led from one thing to the other until he met Chief Samuel Mutero and *Gogo* Ndoro, and the impact that had on his life; the connection with his Jewish heritage. To him, these were men and women who lived their creeds. They did not only preach love but dedicated their lives to putting virtue into action. They showed their followers how things were done. They led from the front.

It was not only their sermons that were very wise and true, but they let their followers get their lessons by observing their daily lives. There was congruence between what they said on one hand and their actions, and how they lived on the other hand. As leaders, they were like the scaffolds that he had envisioned while standing at London Bridge. They helped him see the world differently and to regain his perspective. Suddenly, he thought of the words of Clare Finding and realised that, although Clare's words had given him a vision in big strokes, his journey of faith with the chiefs had carried him through the detail and along that journey he felt that he had indeed been trained for life.

The end